The Last
Wall

Steve Paul

i

The Last Wall

Edited by Jake George www.sagewordservices.com

Printed by Sage Words Publishing
www.sagewordspublishing.com

Cover artwork by ID 40859240 Anderm
Dreamstime.com

Cover design by Jake George, Sage Words Services

ISBN- 978-1-7329182-2-1

Dedication

I would like to dedicate this book to my wife Judy, for her help and encouragement.

I would also like to thank Jake George, owner of Sage Words Publishing, for publishing The Last Wall, my fifth book with him

Steve Paul

October, 2018

Chapter One

The leader, Abd al- Rashid, walked down the side of a stone wall towards the camp where a hundred and thirty men stood by their horses and camels. The Janjaweed were ready to move out, weapons ready, supplies loaded in wagons and only waiting for words from the man approaching them, a long sword at his side and a rifle slung on his back.

The Janjaweed were made up of Sudanese Arab tribes, most of who were from the groups of camel and cattle herding people. They were at odds with Darfur's natives who farmed land taking away ground used for grazing. As rainfall lessened, water became scarce – land used for grazing dried up when the available water was used for the crops. However, most of the Janjaweed were nomads and experienced fighters, not concerned with the land or the water, just the spoils from destroying villages and killing the inhabitants.

It was thought the Sudanese Government, or at least some high ranking officials, backed the Janjaweed, and allowed genocide of the natives because of religious differences.

Abd al- Rashid climbed onto a metal ammo box. "We leave in an hour to find glory. Glory in taking the land, and killing the ones who are the so called Christians. They have denied our demands to give us their land and to denounce their Christian faith. For this they will die. We begin at Tarfiah and move south until there are no villages left. Allah Akbar!" He raised his

1

rifle as the men cheered and raised their weapons. "Death to the infidels, strength to our cause," he shouted.

* * *

The Janjaweed rode for six days to the east until they crested a ridge at the beginning of nightfall overlooking the village. Cook fires could be seen glowing around the huts, while figures strolled to and from the huts. Tarfiah was settled near a small body of water that glistened in the setting sun, long shadows stretched over the village from the ridge. An aura of peace settled over the village and if one listened closely, one could hear songs being sung thanking their god for a blessing of crops.

Abd al- Rashid held his left hand high into the air and pulled a curved sword with his other hand. Without a word, he pointed the sword towards the village and spurred his horse into a run down the ridge, followed by his men. A dust cloud formed from the hooves of the camels and horses running full out down the dry dirt ridge.

A farmer named Hinsel, tall and lanky, carried a bucket of water towards one of the cooking fires. He cocked his head and looked to the ridge. Dropping the bucket he ran towards the center of the village, screaming, "Run, run for your lives! Janjaweed!" He reached his hut grabbing his son and daughter who were playing outside the entrance, yelling at his wife inside the hut to run. Hinsel, with a child under each arm, turned as he heard screams and yells filled with panic. He dropped the two children as a man shoved a spear into his chest and pushed him to the ground. A sword blade cut into his neck, severing his spine. He died before seeing the Janjaweed fighter kill his children with his sword.

The village and fields burned after the massacre. Wagons pulled with horses were loaded with food from the huts. Bodies lay scattered on the ground… men, women and children. No one had been spared.

Two hours later, along a small watering hole, Abd al- Rashid halted the fighters, and told them to make camp. Setting guards out on the perimeter, he said to the assembled men, "There are more villages we will destroy, because Allah demands it. We will rest and celebrate our victory tonight. After that, we ride south."

He assembled the lieutenants inside his tent, laid a map on the floor rug, then with a pencil in his hand marked a route they were going to take. "We will keep the men satisfied by giving them wine, and taking women for their use before killing them." He grinned, "Allah rewards us."

Chapter Two

Jean Paul Allahamba slammed the door as he entered his office, his hand running over a deep frown on his face. On the wall were plaques, trophies and pictures of him with celebrities and politicians. A portrait hanging against the far wall showed a smiling Jean Paul in a New York Knicks uniform. Allahamba had been the highest paid NBA player for six years, where rather than becoming the spoiled, super rich athlete the newspapers headlined for drug use, breaking the law and buying mansions, he quietly invested his money and learned the communications business by interning in the off-seasons. He eventually bought a failing broadcast company, changed the venue to world news, hired bright newscasters and the rest was history. WBC now stood second in the viewing polls with the big four.

The office was on the fifty-fourth floor of the Dunlap building. World Broadcast Company headquarters took the last four floors of the building, and on the floors below were Fidelity Investments, Bloomington On-Line, and of course, Dunlap Tires, LTD.

Five flat screen TV's were on the south wall, all on the news channels: CNN, NBC, CBS, ABC, and not unexpectedly, his station, WBC. The headlining story of the hour was the Janjaweed militia continuing to invade villages in Darfur, a region on Sudan's western border with Chad. Armed by the Sudanese Arabic government, the Janjaweed systematically killed, raped and looted in every village they invaded, though the government denied the allegations. It was reported the entire issue was over natural grazing grounds and farmlands as water became scarce. The Africans were using what the Janjaweed said was theirs. However, many experts claimed the Janjaweed were fighting a religious war, Muslim Arabs against Christian black Africans, and the Janjaweed were winning. The death toll was unknown as news agencies weren't allowed in the country. Messages sneaked out told of massacres and natives forced into slavery.

A map on CNN showed the route the Janjaweed were moving, south in the direction of the village Kumkjeri, Jean Paul's birthplace and where his family still lived and his father had died. Jean Paul had brought one brother to the U.S. years ago, but his mother and two sisters wouldn't leave their homeland. Too soon, possibly in six weeks or less, the horse and camel riding Janjaweed militia would probably arrive to destroy the village and kill as many inhabitants as they could.

Something had to be done. Appealing to the African Union peace keeping force brought nothing but wasted time, empty promises, and continued death to the Africans of Darfur. Having tried all legal channels to no avail, Allahamba decided it was time to take matters into his own hands to somehow keep his family and village safe. With a net worth of over twelve billion dollars, Jean Paul thought he should be able to change destiny. He just had to be very careful in how he attempted to do this.

* * *

"You wanted to see me, Jean Paul?" asked Logan McCutchen, walking into the office.

"Sit down, Logan. Have you been watching the news about Darfur?"

McCutchen nodded his head as Allahamba continued, "I'm about to break some laws, here and internationally. First, let me tell you what I have in mind."

McCutchen was head of security for Jean Paul. He was a former NYPD detective until February 26, 1993, when a bomb went off in the lower parking garage of the north building of the World Trade Center, killing six and injuring one thousand. He resigned on the twenty-eighth of February, enlisted in the Army the same day, and after basic, graduated from the Airborne school then volunteered for the Rangers. He had been assigned to the 3rd Battalion of the 75th Ranger Regiment. In April of 2006 an IED went off next to his Hummer, blowing his lower right arm and hand to pieces scattering the blood and bone down the street of the Iraqi city of Sadr City. Two years later he retired with the rank of captain and began drinking away the memories.

Jean Paul met him when recruiting veterans for his businesses at a half-way house in New York. When he saw the personality and intelligence of the man, he hired him with the provision Logan would attend a program Jean Paul had for wounded vets. The program had the top psychologists and psychiatrists specializing in PTSD. After months of intensive therapy, and a new prosthetic hand and lower arm, McCutchen was released and started work for the company. On his first day of work he told Jean Paul his life had been saved by the man.

McCutchen sat in a leather chair to the side of the desk, a puzzled look on his face. "Fire away."

Ten minutes later, Jean Paul finished his narrative. "There's risk of prison, maybe getting killed. If you don't feel we can do this, say so. I would like you to run the operation, either from here or with us."

"What do mean, 'with us?'"

"I'm going also. There is nothing I would ask someone to do that I won't do myself, and it's my family," he said, picking up a photograph from his desk and held it out to Logan. "My mother and both sisters."

"You're sure as hell not going to try this without me, Jean Paul. Let me do some research, check some things out and I would like to discuss this with a very good, knowledgeable friend." McCutchen could guess his boss's objection as Jean Paul frowned. "I trust him with my life, in fact I have several times. You don't have to worry about him not being totally confidential. My word on it."

Allahamba held his hand up like a cop stopping traffic. He lowered it and looked at a photograph sitting on his desk of a family in traditional African festival garb. "I need to be blunt. Can you put yourself in that kind of situation again?"

"Six years is a long time to heal. I'm fine, ask the docs."

"All right, Logan. Remember, time is of the essence."

* * *

Four days later, McCutchen walked into Jean Paul's office carrying a briefcase. Allahamba stood up from his desk and said, "You have a plan?" The look on his face brought a smile to McCutchen as he sat down.

"If you have the political pull, which we think you should, there's a possibility we can save the village. But," he said, motioning Allahamba to not interrupt, "it means killing as many Janjaweed as possible. Actually, wipe the whole goddamn militia that attacks the village off the face of the earth." He paused for a moment, then said, "Are you prepared for that? Brutal death, killing by any means possible and available."

Jean Paul formed a steeple with his fingers under his chin. "I'm a Christian. Raised that way since a child in Kumkjeri. My mother prays every night for the safety of her children. You say the only way to save the people of the village is by killing the Janjaweed, at least for the present." He took a deep breath. "You're damn right I can do it. You start getting things set on your side and I'll do my part with the political arrangements."

McCutchen slid a paper across the desk. "This is what we'll need, it's going to cost you a lot of money. I'm going to need my friend, a man who served under me in Iraq, to see about getting us the equipment and help in recruiting the manpower. It might be a bit sticky for you in getting him, but like I said, I need him. After that, give us two weeks to a month."

* * *

A day later, it began. "Mr. Allahamba, Senator Feltor is here," the secretary said over the intercom.

"Send him in, and bring us coffee; cream and sugar for the Senator."

Senator Feltor, chairman of the Armed Forces Appropriations Committee, and member of the Senate Intelligence Committee, walked into the office with his hat in his hand. "Jean Paul, how nice to see you."

"Please, sit down, Terry." After Feltor sat in a chair in front of the massive desk, Allahamba put a sheet of paper on the desk in front of him. "I need your influence and help to pull some strings for an operation I'm starting."

"Want to make another billion, do you? You're talking something legal, aren't you?" Feltor said with a chuckle. He stirred cream and sugar in his coffee and took a tentative sip. "What do you need?"

"I have family living in Darfur... a village of about two hundred natives. They're in grave danger from the Janjaweed militia who are advancing towards the village. I'm sure you know the African Union isn't any help so I'm getting a force together, call them mercenaries if you will, to stop them."

"Whoa, just hold on a minute, Jean Paul. You can't do that. We would have to have Sudan's permission to bring troops into the country. And we don't have any treaties with Sudan. Hell, if we did the Marines would go in and take care of the rebels. No, no way. Sorry."

Allahamba stood up and walked around the desk to the side of the senator with the sheet of paper in his hand. "We've been through a lot together, haven't we, Terry."

"We sure have, Jean Paul, and I appreciate everything you've—"

"Stop. Now. This is the amount of money I've contributed to you and your reelection committee. This is the amount of money you have taken from me and travelled over the world for your personal pleasure. This," he pointed to a name, "is the woman you've had an affair with over the last fourteen months. Should I continue?"

"No," Feltor said. "Do you know what you're requesting me to do? I don't know how many international and United Nation treaties that would be broken."

"Terry, I don't care. I'm not supporting rebels, or going to overthrow the government, just save my family and their village." He put another paper down. "This is what I need from you: access to Satellite surveillance for these coordinates, intelligence from the CIA on the Janjaweed, and passports for my men without any interference from the government."

The senator had turned a pasty white. "Is that all?"

"No. Two more items. The name on the bottom, Shelby Donavan, is in prison at the Lewisburg Federal Prison in Pennsylvania."

"What's he in for, mass murder?" Feltor licked his lips with his tongue and a sickly smile spread over his face.

"He was a Ranger and was hurt in Sadr City. When he recovered from his wounds, he left the army and later went into selling weapons to a rebel group in Somalia. He was caught with a ship full of guns and rocket launchers leaving a Texas shipping port. Got sentenced to fifteen years. I also need for you to have this satellite phone reach my sister in the village of Kumkjeri. I don't care how you get it to her."

"My God, Jean Paul. You expect me to do all this?"

"Yes, yes I do. You're a powerful senator with a lot of influence and connections. Make the arrangements to get Donavan out of prison by the end of the week. Terry, know this, I have never been so serious about anything else in my life. I will do anything, spend everything, to save my family and the village."

"Why don't you just bring them over here. I can easily get visas for them."

"And the two hundred villagers?"

"I could try, but probably not." Feltor stood and faced Allahamba. "I want your word if I can do this, you'll give me everything you have regarding the business we've done."

"My word, Terry."

"Whatever happens, after this is over, you'll continue to support me as a senator, financially. Is that agreeable?"

"Deliver what I need, and we'll continue our political relationship. My man in prison is your first priority. Please keep me informed, Senator Feltor."

* * *

Four days later, on a cold, snow blown day, Shelby Donavan left the Lewisburg Federal Prison. When the gate closed behind him, he took a deep breath of freedom and held his arms up in the air. A black Chevrolet Tahoe was parked in front of the release gate, motor running. Donavan walked to the SUV, opened the back door and looked in.

"Logan! What a grand surprise."

Chapter Three

"Shelby, get in. We have a lot to talk about, my friend," McCutchen said.

"I see you now have a hand to be able to shake with. Congratulations. Obviously you've turned your life around."

"Thanks to a special person," McCutchen replied... He went on to tell Donavan about his history and relationship with Jean Paul Allahamba, and the extent of his loyalty to him, saying he would even kill to protect his boss. He then told him of the plan and what they needed from Donavan: weapons and transportation logistics. Also, if he knew men who could be trusted and interested in the operation. Military or ex-military. A limited group of twenty-five to thirty men.

"We'll need enough weapons to arm the locals, if they'll fight. And I don't know that they won't run first," McCutchen said. "It won't be the first time where the fighting's been left up to us, will it? Even though it cost me a hand and you a leg."

"No, and some unpleasant memories wondering where the hell our backup was hiding. You have a big order for the amount of time you've given me. But I am grateful, Captain, and you getting me out of that shit-hole gives me an enormous amount of motivation. Okay, so what's the budget?"

"Get the material, we'll take care of the payments. Shelby, you and I survived the IED when the two soldiers in the back seat didn't. We're brothers in blood, so remember, you're going to get paid a hell of a lot of money for this, more if you join us in the fighting, don't pad the ticket. Are we on the same wave length, my friend?" McCutchen said.

"Brothers in blood. I like that," Donavan said. He put his hand out and said, "Use that new hand and give me a shake."

McCutchen put his hand out and the two men shook, then Donavan leaned in and put his arms around his ex-squad leader. "I'm putting my trust and life in your real hand and the phony one. But, you know, that thing feels half real, looks pretty good too."

McCutchen patted Donovan's leg. "That's a good looking new leg you got. I couldn't see you limp when you walked to the car. It's the highest tech prosthesis made, almost like the Bionic Man."

"I'm forever grateful to you and Mr. Allahamba."

"You ever think we'd be getting into something like this again? Going off to fight? Maybe not coming back?" Logan asked, looking out the window.

"I didn't." Donavan rubbed his leg and shook his head. "I'm just glad you remembered your pal, or as you said, brother in blood."

* * *

As they drove towards the Lewisburg airport, Logan's cell phone rang. He answered and talked softy for a few minutes then pushed the end button.

"Good news or bad?" Donavan asked. He stared out the back window watching the prison disappear behind him. He could hardly believe his good luck in getting out. The three years he'd spent had been some of the worst of his life. Not in the sense of the violence that was always possible in the dark alcoves and hallways, but being subject to the orders of the authorities, and his freedom being a memory. The loss of his freedom was so strong he made a silent vow he would never again go back to prison, no matter what it would entail.

"Good. Someone I know is going to help us behind the scenes. This is lucky for us, Shelby. The guy has a position in the U.S. intelligence community and is outraged at the genocide going on over there."

"I'm happy for us. Where are we going now?"

"New York. Jean Paul wants to meet you in person. He's smart and down to earth. Not a typical multi-millionaire." McCutchen held his hand up. "Before you ask, he owns a broadcast company. WBC. He's Sudanese, from a village in Darfur."

"Ah, that makes sense, now. I wondered why the militia thing for a place that's been in civil war for years. Does he really thing he can make a difference? I mean, eventually, most of the natives will be gone or dead."

McCutchen told him Jean Paul's long term goal was to save the village which would in turn save his remaining family. Hopefully he could force world attention on the Janjaweed committing genocide for the Arabic government. "I really think he wants to put an end to the terror by force, rather than talk. Every day this goes on he gets more pissed since all the peace keepers like the United Nations and Africa Union, talk of intervention and yet haven't stopped a damn thing. Always some reason or another."

They arrived at the airport and pulled up to a hangar at the end of the terminal. A Learjet 40 with the logo, WBC on the tail sat on the tarmac. The passenger door opened and steps dropped down when the Tahoe pulled up to the hanger.

Boarding the jet, Shelby saw a tall, casually dressed black man sitting near the back of the passenger cabin stand up.

"Please," the man said, "sit here, Mr. Donavan," pointing to the seat next to him.

Donavan sat down offering his hand. "Mr. Allahamba, I presume."

McCutchen took a seat near the front of the plane as the speakers in the ceiling advised everyone to buckle up and prepare for takeoff. The jet taxied to the end of the runway, throttles opened, and the Lear headed down the runway increasing speed, then lifting off the ground. The retracting wheels made a loud rumble for a quick moment.

"Logan told you why we had you released from prison. Along with that, an offer for you to help us besides procuring the arms." Allahamba asked.

Donavan said he'd been told why and appreciated the offer to help. And, yes, he would fight with them. Allahamba nodded and opened a small compartment in front of him. "Care for a drink? Probably your first one in three years."

Donavan waved it off. "Not right now, thanks. I'll have some when I get settled in a place."

McCutchen had come back when the jet leveled off and sat in the seats facing the two men. Pulling an envelope out of his coat pocket, he handed it to Donavan. "Keys to an apartment. In the bathroom closet is a briefcase with cash and a cell phone that is untraceable. Anything else you need, we'll provide it. My cell number," he handed over a piece of paper. "Also untraceable."

"You have an interesting background, Mr. Donavan," Allahamba said. "The government has a file on you without too much information in it. Mostly suspicions of supplying weapons to different groups. Apparently you were caught because of an informant. We don't want someone informing to be a problem."

"What can I say?" Donavan said. " I hear the informant was found dead a short time later. He ratted me off for money so I don't have a lot of sympathy. Here's the thing, Mr. Allahamba;" Pausing for a moment, he seemed to collect his thoughts. "In all probability I can get the weapons needed, some transportation, and hell, even some ex-Rangers who will be happy to fight the good fight. But I have a feeling this could easily end up being another 'Blackhawk Down,' if you know what I'm talking about. These Arab fighters are tough and crazy, especially if they're fighting a religious war."

Allahamba took a sip of his drink and looked out the jet's window. "I've never been in war or any situation where I could die violently. It's scary as hell. But I also love my mother and sisters and I am willing to sacrifice myself to make them safe. I guess, Shelby, we need men who don't really care if they live or die. Soldiers who are at a loss because they aren't fighting for a cause. Does that make sense? Selfish as this seems on my part." Allahamba took a handkerchief out of his shirt pocket and wiped his eyes. "Allergies," he said, with a sad smile. "This mission won't have rules against the enemy."

"Yeah, it makes sense, Jean Paul, and I'm impressed. Can I call you Jean Paul?"

"Please do, I'm honored."

The speaker came on announcing for everyone to fasten their seatbelts, landing at Newark International Airport in seven minutes. They could feel the deceleration of the jet and a few minutes later the rumble of the landing gear going down. The jet landed and taxied to a hangar at the end of the concourses.

As the jet pulled next to the hanger, Donavan said, "Logan, Jean Paul, did you ever see the movie, The Magnificent Seven?"

Logan nodded his head and Jean Paul said no.

"Watch the movie," Donavan said, getting up from his seat.

* * *

McCutchen and Allahamba left the airport in a chauffeur driven Lincoln Town Car, taking the less traveled Inner-Highway. "Your thoughts, " Jean Paul asked.

"He'll do the job. To be on the safe side I'll have some of my security crew keep a watch out, in case someone from the government takes an interest in him. Is there something bothering you about Shelby?"

"He doesn't seem to be nearly as serious about this as I would have thought. He's almost flippant. Logan, we're talking about going to a country where there isn't any law and the government is at the very least, condoning murder and rape of Africans, and my God, he's telling me to watch a movie! He isn't what I expected. I wonder if we made a mistake getting him."

Logan smiled. "Jean Paul, when our Hummer got hit with the IED, he and I were both blown to hell. My hand, his leg, not much left. The two guys in back were shredded. Actually, their bodies took the main blast and shielded us from the brunt of the IED. We got out and somehow made it to a ditch on the side of the road. We had to put tourniquets on each other because we were bleeding like stuck hogs. A half-dozen Mahdi militia were coming up the road, yelling for us to surrender. If we'd been taken prisoner, who knows what would have happened, so Shelby puts my M4 in my good hand and wraps the sling so I can fire the rifle and not drop it.

"Now, Jean Paul, this is Shelby. He'd brought another rifle so he's holding two M4's. One in each hand. He says, 'Logan, you ever see 'Butch Cassidy and the Sundance Kid?' And I say, What? Are you crazy, who gives a shit. He says because we're gonna do what Butch and Sundance did at the end of the movie. Using his one good leg, he drags me up with him and says, 'Let's give'm hell, Sundance,' and we started shooting. No running, no ducking for cover, just firing as fast as we can. Killed every damn one of them. He says, 'Good work, now get some help,' and passes out. Never brought up that he saved my life other than tell me not to tell anyone what happened in the ditch."

McCutchen took a deep breath. "You're the only person I've told since then. I think he made a good point. See the movie."

* * *

The apartment was nice. Not flashy, more like cozy. Inside the bathroom closet was the briefcase with cash and the cell phone. He smiled when he saw the small bar stocked with mini-bottles of vodka and bourbon with beer and mix in the fridge. After pouring vodka and tonic over a glass of ice cubes, he hummed to himself while dialing a number on the cell phone.

When the phone was answered he said, "I'm in New York." He gave the address, took a sip of the drink, then said, "How soon can you be here? Excellent, see you then and keep an eye out, Sam." He pushed the end button, grinned, and decided to have another drink or two.

Chapter Four

A rusty motorcycle entered the village of Kumkjeri ridden by a man with goggles over his eyes and wearing a dirty shirt and pants. His entire body was covered in a soft blanket of brown dust. He parked the bike and asked a curious boy where the tribal elder was, then slung a canvas rucksack over his shoulder and followed the boy to a hut made of mud mixed in with straw. Entering, he saw an older man standing in a corner next to a younger woman.

The rider bowed his head for a moment in respect, then said, "You should make plans to leave soon, the Janjaweed are on their way. They've already raided and set fire to Ahdar Sadal and Tama Hileh. It's terrible, I don't know how many women and children were raped and killed, but I found one woman, who said twenty men had raped her. She was nearly dead. This was two weeks ago, near Hlil. There's no hope except to flee to Chad."

The elder frowned and said, "The border to Chad is closed because there's been too many of our people crossing into their country for safety. The refugee camps are overflowing. The conditions are terrible."

"We need to stand and fight," the younger woman said, standing up, fists clenched. "The SLA is in the mountains. I'll go find them and see if they will protect us, or at least help us defend ourselves."

"Don't bother. I'm a member. We've been ordered to defend Rongai Taba. It's too large of a village to let the Janjaweed destroy it. They've split forces with

19

nearly a hundred fighters coming here. The larger force is going to raid Rongai Taba. I'm sorry, but we can't help you. The Arab Muslims want to get rid of all our villages. You have only a few weeks to flee. God help us." As if remembering why he carried the rucksack, he asked, "I need to find a woman by the name of Aafreen Allahamba. Do you know her?"

"Why do you want her?" the woman asked.She slid away from the elder, bent down, then raised back up, her hand under some folds of her toub, the traditional Sudanese women's clothing which was yards of cloth wrapped around their bodies.

"I have a package to deliver."

The tribal elder held his hand out. "Give it to me, I'll see she gets it."

The rider shook his head. "I can't give this to anyone but Aafreen Allahamba."

"I'm Aafreen. Who sent it to me?"

He shook his head again. "I don't know. A man came to our camp yesterday and told the commander he wanted the package delivered to you. The commander does what the man wants when he comes. That's all I know." He opened the rucksack and took out a box taped shut and a wax seal on the box flaps.

She held the box in her hand, set it on the floor, then put her hand on the arm of the rider and said, "Thank you and God keep you safe." After he left she took the pistol out from her toub, set in on a basket, then ripped the box open taking out a letter and cell phone. Reading the letter, she looked up and said, "It's from my brother in the United States. I have to call him," she said to the confused looking elder, leaving the tent.

Aafreen was the type of woman who was outspoken and didn't agree with being silent because she was female. Never married, she questioned actions by the men of the tribe, recommended changes, and was basically what in the USA, would be called a woman's libber. She was largely ignored.

She walked to her mother's hut wondering if her father would have lived, would things be different? Maybe, maybe not, but no use dwelling on the past because it made no difference now. Entering the hut, Aafreen saw her sister, Cabriol, helping her mother on the handloom, holding a small ball of cotton yarn in hands misshapen from rheumatoid arthritis.

Her mother looked up and said, "What do you have?" then bent back over the loom, her feet pushing the lathe.

"A letter from Jean Paul, a satellite phone, solar charger, and money," Aafreen answered, drawing the letter out of the box. "Give me a minute to read it."

Aafreen was the only one of the family who could read. Christian missionaries saw her intelligence years ago when they worked with the village natives for several months. The missionaries roamed Africa for centuries converting the Sudanese to Christianity. Missionaries were in the village when the mother was born, and had insisted she be named Grace, which stood for grace of God.

"I have to call him." She squinted at the phone and poked the numbers in. The last thing was hitting the green "call" button. Seconds passed, then her face lit up. "Jean Paul, what in the world is this?"

She listened intently for several minutes while Grace and Cabriol came over to her saying, "We want to talk to Jean Paul. Share the phone."

Aafreen held her hand up. "Shush, please. Just for a minute more." She nodded her head as she listened into the satellite phone. "Yes, yes Jean Paul. I will do my best. Here's Mother and Cabriol." Grace took the phone from her.

"My son!" she said leaning close to Cabriol so they both could hear and talk. The two women were animated as they talked to the son and brother for ten minutes. Finally, Grace handed the phone to Aafreen.

"I'll talk to Omallia, and we'll meet with the men. Yes, I know, and we will do our best. I'll call you in two days. God be with you." She pushed the "end" button and put the phone back into the box. "Did he tell you?" Aafreen asked her mother. Grace shook her head.

"He's coming home... to protect us."

* * *

Omallia had grown up with Aafreen, the childhood friend. When asked why they didn't marry he would reply she was too strong of a woman, one who would never walk two steps behind her husband and do as he commanded. "She would throw me to the lions if I tried to keep her quiet and at home," he would tell his friends. But he did love the woman and was sure he would follow her to battle the devil, if needed. He had been strong willed also, and as a younger man had fought with the Sudan Liberation Army in the second civil war of south Sudan. During a battle, Omallia was captured by the Army of Sudan, later beaten, tortured, and left for dead in an overcrowded stockade. During a moonless, pitch black night, he dug under the fence deep enough to slid his emaciated body through and made his way back to Kumkjeri in a journey that took two weeks. When he showed up at the village, his six foot, four inch frame weighed one-hundred-twenty-eight pounds. He still carried a deep fear of being back in a stockade as a prisoner.

He looked up and smiled when he heard Aafreen calling his name before she walked around a hut and saw him. When he saw the look on her face, his smile disappeared. "What?"

She came up close to him and said, "We have to have a meeting with the tribe." Telling Omallia about her call, she finished by saying, "Jean Paul is bringing weapons and soldiers. He wants us to find as many villagers as we can who will fight the Janjaweed with him and the soldiers."

"What's the matter?" Aafreen said, seeing Omallia draw back from her. It seemed as if sweat broke out on his forehead in that instant.

"You want old men and a few young ones to fight against the Janjaweed? We'll be slaughtered."

"Women can fight too!"

"Hah. You're trying to live a dream. We have to leave, get to safety somewhere," Omallia wiped his face with his shirt tail. An odor of fear crept off his body. He reached for her.

Aafreen pushed him away. "Don't. You might not have the will to fight, but by the God, I know many of us who will," she said, raising her chin up and staring at him with a piercing gaze.

"Your father died trying to negotiate with the Arab government. Have you forgotten so soon?" he asked.

"No, I haven't." She remembered the pain when learning of his death. He had been the tribal elder and had taken it upon himself to try for a peaceful settlement with the government. They took him, killed him, and hung his body from a lamp pole . The government denied any responsibility for the murder, blaming insurgents. No one was ever charged.

"But I'm not talking negotiation with a government. I'm telling you we can fight the Janjaweed and defeat them with my brother's help. If we show them we are not going to allow our village to be destroyed, our children and women not to be raped and murdered, there won't be a price too high to pay."

She looked again at Omallia again and her face softened. Her hand went to his face, gently.

"Don't," he said, stepping back. "You can't speak for anyone but yourself. Do you realize you are asking people to die for huts and livestock, when they can escape now, to Chad, or somewhere else where it will be safe?"

Aafreen lowered her hand and with a sad shake of her head, said, "Ask the elder about Chad, ask who will welcome us to their country. Even now, refugees are living in filth, living in camps, probably like the stockade you were in." She stuck her chin out. "Not for me. I'll fight with whoever will join Jean Paul and his men." Again, she reached for him. "Will you fight with us?"

This time he allowed her to touch his face. "There will have to be a plan, one that the tribe will support. The old and children will need to get as far south as possible for their safety, and take the livestock with them."

"Will you have the elder call for a meeting tonight? Time can't be wasted."

He nodded his head.

* * *

The men gathered around the fire questioning Omallia. A murmur sounded when Aafreen and twelve women joined the meeting.

"You shouldn't be here," one man said. "We are going to discuss things that men decide, not women."

"Let her speak," Omallia said. "You know she won't be quiet anyway." There was a chuckle around the fire.

Aafreen stood up and told of the Janjaweed coming, her brother's pledge of help and the women with her who had sworn to fight. Three times, someone had tried to interrupt but she silenced them with a wave of her hand and the look of scorn on her face. "Jean Paul is bringing extra weapons for us. No matter what you decide to do, we women are going to take the weapons and fight. Enough is enough." She turned and the other women followed her out of the meeting.

A man known as Koutana, raised to his feet. "This is an insult, a woman speaking to us that way, saying they are going to fight. We should leave the village as soon as possible."

The tribal elder stood. "She's right. If Aafreen was a man everyone would be agreeing to stay and defend our people and village. Everyone stand up," he ordered. All the men stood, some looking at the ground, not facing the elder.

"Every man who will fight with the women and me, come over here." He dragged his foot through the dirt making a long line. "Anyone who won't, stay where you are."

When they were finished, five men, including Koutana, stayed where they had been. "You will take the rest of the tribe and the livestock, south, where it will be your duty to keep everyone safe. We will give you supplies, a weapon for each man, and accompany you for a few days," the elder told Koutana. To the men who had crossed the line, he said, "You are courageous, God will be on our side."

All total, twenty-four men and thirteen women would fight with Jean Paul and his soldiers. God be with them.

Chapter Five

There was a soft knock on the apartment's door just before the wall clock struck one in the morning. Shelby rose from the couch, moved to the door and asked who was there.

"Sam. Everything looks cool, let me in."

He unlocked the door, opened it quickly, put a bear hug around Sam and said, "God, I've missed you."

"How on earth did you get out? When we talked last week you didn't say anything. Kind of pisses me off, you rat." She began taking her clothes off. "Com'on, Shelby, I've missed you." She flipped her panties to the floor with one foot and walked to the bedroom.

"To quote an old saying, 'You don't have to tell me twice,'" Shelby said, unbuttoning his shirt as he followed her into the room.

* * *

The sun shining through the window woke Shelby up. He put a hand over his eyes, felt to his side, and smiled when his hand fell on Sam's shoulder. "Wake up, kid, we've got work to do and not a hell of a lot of time to do it."

"I was awake, just looking at you," she said. Pulling the sheet to her neck and sitting up in the bed, Samantha Pershing, daughter of Benjamin Pershing, owner of World Imports and Exports LLP, also supplier of rifles, rocket launchers, transportation and training for anyone who could pay, covered a smile with her hand. "Daddy says hello."

"You told him I got out? Didn't I tell you to keep this quiet until I gave the okay?" Shelby climbed out of bed and put his pants on. "Damn, Sam, I'm glad you did, it'll save us time."

"Don't plan on getting back in bed, Shelby. We have a lot to do."

"I know. You can't understand how much I'm looking forward to this, especially after three years of sitting in a cell."

After Shelby had been through the ordeal of losing his leg, then getting a prosthetic one, it only took a short period of time until he was able to walk with it, though with a pronounced limp. He left Walter Reed with a feeling of needing motivation to fulfill his life. He didn't want an eight to five job, with a wife and children. No, that wasn't for him, he wanted adventure. Something to raise his blood pressure wondering if he could survive whatever challenge he faced. He had loved being in battles, and he wanted more, so he could feel life. Shelby wanted the feeling of pure adrenalin flowing through his body, wanted where a single decision could make a difference of life or death. Something without politics dictating how or who you could kill if they were the enemy.

He made coffee and brought two cups to the kitchen table, where Sam sat down, showered and dressed, a notebook in front of her. As they drank the coffee, he told her what they were going to need, where it would be going, not sure the amount of weapons, oh and by the way he would be going also.

"What's the budget?" She asked, not taking the bait of the last sentence.

"However much it takes. We don't want to go cheap or skimp on the quantity," he said. "Benjamin should be able to get us everything, don't you think?"

"Of course. Will you take the merchandise or have it delivered somewhere over there?"

"Delivered, if possible. Sam, before you tell me not to go, I need this, especially after being in prison. So don't even try to talk me out of it. Deal?" Shelby stuck his hand out. When she ignored him, he put his hand down.

"I knew you would and it never crossed my mind you shouldn't. Daddy will have to see how we can get the merchandise either close or to the village. Maybe through the Central African Republic. They're fighting Islamist rebels so I think that's our key. Going to Darfur to fight some Islamists," Sam said, her forehead lined from concentration.

Shelby smiled at her. When he'd been in physical rehab, she worked at her profession as a psychologist at the facility. Therapy sessions with the vets, bringing and writing letters, sitting for hours listening to the stories, fears, and ambitions of the wounded, she began spending more time with him. They went on tours around the city, then dinners, then making love. Shelby had fallen in love with her. He found out after proclaiming his love, Samantha also recruited a very select few men to train rebels in different countries of Africa. Not the religious radicals, or al-Qaeda-linked groups, but the countrymen who had formed to fight for their lives and rights against dictators and authoritarian governments. Something Shelby found an immediate interest in doing.

Shelby had all the qualifications required to train guerrilla forces. He told her he wanted to be involved and didn't care where he went, except not the Middle East, and not as a contractor for the US government.

Several months later he found himself in the northwest region of Somalia, helping train guerrilla soldiers for the Somali Salvation Democratic Front. It was an adventure for him. Staying in touch with Samantha, she asked if he'd be interested in working with her father, Benjamin Pershing, supplying weapons to the rebels.

At first he declined, then after a price was put on his head and nearly getting killed by some of the rebels he was training, he decided selling military weapons to the increasing number of guerrillas forces was a better choice. The new profession had given him a reasonable amount of adventure, time with Sam, and money. His life took a sudden turn when he was arrested by the FBI as he was getting ready to board a container ship filled with weapons bound for Somalia, and sentenced to federal prison for gun smuggling.

Sam put the notebook in the pocket of her jacket. "I'm going to see what Daddy can do for us and I'll call you later."

"Dinner at Rocco's tonight?"

"Sure, I'll come over around eight if that works for you," she said.

"You need to get a phone that can't be traced."

She dug a cell phone out of her coat. "It's what you called me on yesterday." She stood up, put on her jacket and said, "See you later," as the door closed behind her.

* * *

Logan McCutchen answered his Tracfone on the second ring. "What do you have, Shelby?"

"I need numbers. How many rifles, pistols and odd assortment of weapons will we need?"

"We have, so far, eighteen ex-US military and thirty-seven villagers. We're working on getting some more soldiers. Have you found anyone?" McCutchen asked, then held his breath waiting for Shelby to squeal.

He waited, exhaled, then took another breath. "Shelby?"

"Tell me you're shitting me, Logan. Isn't this a bit of an optimistic view on what fifty some-odd men can do. Thirty-seven of them goat herders who probably haven't done a lot of shooting at someone. And no, I haven't found anyone yet since I just got to town last night, if you remember, and as a first priority, I'm securing weapons for us, unless you've forgotten."

"Cattle," Logan said.

"What?"

"They herd cattle, not goats."

Shelby laughed until he had to stop and catch his breath. If McCutchen could have seen him, he would have seen tears running down his cheeks. "Excuse me, cattle herders." He went off on another fit of laughter.

"What are you going to get for us?"

"Ahhh, okay. AK-47's, the best for reliability, some RPGs, pistols of course, .30 caliber machine guns, transportation and if possible, a nice surprise you'll appreciate. But don't ask what because I'm not sure I can do that one. It's going to cost some big dollars, because of the time element," Shelby said.

"Like I said, don't worry about the cost. Let me know when you need the money. One other thing. I put a couple of my security guys down there to watch your back. They're good, so you shouldn't see them. If there's a problem, call me."

"You don't trust me, Logan?"

"I trust you with my life. That should be enough." McCutchen knew what was coming next.

"Call them off. I'm not going to do this thinking I have to look over my shoulder every minute. Are we clear?" Shelby said, the anger tightening his voice.

"We're clear. I'll get them out of there. I was just trying to make sure you're safe, Shelby. I should have asked you before doing anything. I'm sorry."

"All right, then. I'll get back with you in a day or so, Logan, I'm going to be pretty busy." Shelby ended the call. He called Sam telling her to be aware of anyone who might be following her. He decided not to tell her now about the argument with Logan about his security guys. He would tell her at dinner tonight and they would both be looking over their shoulders.

* * *

FBI special agent Randy Cosworth was mad as hell. A gun supplier he'd put in prison had been released without any warning or notice from the prison. Even in the bureaucratic cesspool of fools who seemed to be appointed to run the show, this shouldn't have happened. When he called the warden, he said an order for release had come from a government agency.

"You are supposed to contact us when anyone's released that's been convicted of supplying arms to rebels. Why didn't you?" Cosworth's face was turning a crimson red from his blood pressure rising dangerously high. He was trying his best not to yell. After a pause from the warden, he said, "What agency?"

"I can't tell you, Agent Cosworth. There was a security clearance."

"SECURITY CLEARANCE! Goddammit, Vickers, I'm an FBI agent. I have clearance."

"Not for this. I can't tell you anymore, Agent Cosworth, Good day." The line went dead.

Cosworth slammed the phone back in its cradle. He called downstairs to the investigative section that handled the division which included Lewisburg,

Pennsylvania. Panting and trying to draw a deep breath, he told the agent answering he wanted Shelby Donavan located. Check the airport, car rentals, anyway he could have left the area. He hung up and took five Tums. The goddamn indigestion was in full speed. Cosworth made a note to himself to see a gastrologist one of these days.

The special agent left the building at a little after six without any progress locating Donavan. A little over three years ago, one of his confidential informants had made it possible for the FBI to make an arrest on the gun smuggler, but when the informant was found dead later, Cosworth took it personally. He knew Donavan had been involved with the death, though he hadn't been able to prove it.

There was no doubt he was into something illegal now, had to be, and when he was caught, Cosworth would stick him so deep in prison no one would ever see him again. That is, if he was captured alive.

Chapter Six

Jean Paul switched his iPad on, fingered in a series of cryptic codes, then his password after the codes were verified. He waited while the satellite images came into focus. After staring at the screen for a few minutes, he cursed under his breath and called McCutchen into his office.

"What's up, Jean Paul?" Logan entered the office. "News from your sister?"

"Look at this and tell me what you think." Jean Paul paced around his office waiting for McCutchen. He was already in a bad mood. His brother, Robert, who he'd brought over to the states years ago, told Jean Paul he was a fool to get involved with the problems of Darfur. Their mother and sisters should leave the village and come here, he'd said. And for the CEO of WBC to even consider going over there himself, was bordering on lunacy. Had arrangements been made to take care of him if Jean Paul was arrested, or, God forbid, killed? Robert didn't realize how fortunate he was that he was thrown out of the office verbally, rather than physically.

"I think the Janjaweed are moving faster than what we thought. It's time to get the recruits together, organize, and cut at least a week off our time frame for landing in Kumkjeri. You might want to call your sister and tell her whoever is leaving the village should start in the next few days," Logan said.

"I'll do that after you and I are finished. Get everyone to the conference room tomorrow afternoon, two o'clock. See if Shelby can make it to give us an update on his acquisitions. I'm taking a leave of absence and putting Phillip Reynolds in charge while I'm gone."

McCutchen looked uneasy then finally said, "What about Robert? Will he cause us any problems?"

"No. He doesn't hold any type of position in the company where he could hurt us. Robert is in charge of building maintenance contracts." Jean Paul shook his head. "He's not too good at that either. Thinks he should be involved in the corporation business. He has the attitude of entitlement based on being my younger brother. I don't know what I did wrong."

Robert had gone to several top business colleges, getting kicked out them all because of poor grades, and at one college, accused of giving a girl the date rape drug. She later dropped charges and Jean Paul thought somehow, Robert had been able to buy her off. In attempting to give Robert all the opportunities Jean Paul's business position and wealth could bring, he had inadvertently contributed to producing a spoiled, unreliable young man.

"So you don't worry, Logan, Phillip has all the legal paperwork making him the interim CEO and not allowing Robert to interfere in the company business," Jean Paul said.

"Good, if I can say it. I'm going to contact the men and arrange transportation for the meeting tomorrow. I'm going to get the sporting goods rep to bring camo hunting clothes and everything needed for an extended hunting trip. We've bought five-thousand MREs from army surplus stores so far, and I think we'll buy some more to leave with the villagers when we're finished, if that's okay with you."

"What about transportation?"

"I'll get with Shelby on that."

Jean Paul picked the iPad up again and stared at the images. "There seems to be more of them that we first thought. I don't know whether to be excited or scared out of my wits."

"Be scared, Jean Paul," Logan said. He left the office leaving one of the richest men in the country knowing he was going to be led, and not the leader, even though he was the man with the money. That was fine with him.

* * *

Two o'clock the next day the conference room had eighteen men, one woman, the CEO of the broadcast company, and the head of company security. Most milled around the room talking with each other. Some were dressed in jackets and slacks, others in jeans and shirts, some clean shaven, fresh haircuts and others, beards and ponytails. The woman was being introduced to the others by Logan McCutchen. Molly Southfield was a physician's assistant, who had been a medic in the 2nd Calvary Regiment, stationed at Kandahar Airfield, Afghanistan for one tour.

Logan stepped up to the front table and said, "Let's get started, if you'll take a seat." He waited for a minute or two while everyone sat down. Shelby Donavan wasn't there. "The Janjaweed are moving faster than what we originally calculated. We think we've lost a week of prep time.

Is everyone here committed?" Several voices said "Sure," " You bet," "Gonna kick some ass." Heads nodded. No one said no.

"As you can see over against the wall are desert camos, boots, jackets, and hats. The helmets and flak jackets, along with the weapons, will be issued when we get into Darfur. We will probably be flying into a neighboring country and we don't want a risk of being caught with military equipment and weapons. The plan now, is to be employees of the World Broadcasting Company going to Darfur to report on the Islamists' war against the natives. There are company clothes with WBC insignias for you, also. Jean Paul will now give you some more info. Jean Paul..."

Before he addressed the group, the door opened and Shelby Donavan entered the room with another man who looked several years older than all the others. Shelby waved to Logan, who headed over to him. Logan held his hand up to Jean Paul. "Just a second, Jean Paul."

"What's going on, Shelby? I was afraid you weren't going to show," Logan said. He looked to the other man and introduced himself. "Logan McCutchen." He held his hand out.

"Lee Prescott," the man said, shaking hands. He had long, gray hair hanging over his collar, an angular face with several days growth of beard, and almost milky blue eyes. Some would say he looked like the actor, Bruce Dern. "Quite the gathering," he said.

"Lee here served two tours in Vietnam as a helicopter pilot. Guess what I got us?" Shelby asked. He had what would be called a shit-eating grin spread across his face. Holding up a hand, he said, "Wait, wait, don't answer. A Russian MI-8T. Can you believe it? 1991 and at a bargain price."

"A helicopter. Great." Logan said. "And you can fly it, Lee?"

"Yup. They're all about the same. Shelby says he can get me a check-ride over there, so nothing to worry about. He's already got a fuel truck lined up."

"Thanks for the information. It's nice someone tells me what's going on with his procurements. You can tell the men what you've got after Jean Paul speaks," Logan said. "Out of curiosity, what country are you getting the equipment and weapons out of?"

"Basically, Ukraine. They have one hell of a network that's going to get the stuff to Darfur,"

Shelby replied. He took a small notebook page out of his pocket and handed it to Logan. "Have

Jean Paul send the money to this Grand Cayman bank account number today. Before you bitch,

you said don't worry about the cost."

Logan's eyebrows raised for a moment, then he motioned to the CEO that he was finished talking to Shelby as he put the paper in his pocket. "Good job."

Jean Paul cleared his throat. "I'll make this brief. You'll be going into battle. Not maybe, there will be one or more battles. Dangerous as anything I'm sure you've experienced, according to Logan McCutchen." He went on to tell them about the Janjaweed, the risks of traveling to the country, and the government corruption.

"We going back to Iraq and Afghanistan?" A voice said, getting some laughter and applause.

Jean Paul smiled. "We're planning on leaving in one week. When you leave, there are some papers for you to sign. Beneficiaries for payment if you don't make it back, disability payments if you're injured. You won't be cheated or your families. You'll be given a copy of the contract guaranteeing payment. You all know Logan. If you have questions or worries about the payment, ask him. Ask a lawyer as long as you don't tell them where we're going or of course, what we're going to do. Rest assured I'm able to pay for your services." He waited to see if anyone had a question, or comment. No one did. "Logan."

"I've arranged for all of you to use The Flintlock Shooting Range in Westwood, New Jersey. They have AR-15s, and semi-auto pistols, so they'll be similar to what we'll have. The passports will be ready day after tomorrow and Jean Paul has leased a small airliner to get us there. If you have any questions or suggestions, talk to me after the meeting. Now Shelby here will tell us the weapons we'll have." He stepped back from the table to make room for Shelby.

"Okay, here's what we're going to have so far. AK-47's, Glock 23's, RPG's, some VEPR Tactical Sniper rifles, and vehicles, some UAZ's that are like a Russian Jeep, a couple of light armored trucks and three cargo trucks. No doubt some of you are wondering why we don't just get some tanks. Well, good idea, but it might be tough to roll through, say, for instance, the Central African Republic, and not have them notice we're driving tanks over the border. You will all receive body armor, night vision goggles radios and the weapons after we cross into Darfur. That's about it, so far." Shelby said. He started to leave, paused, then turned back to the men.

"One last thing. Logan and I fought together in Iraq. That's why I call him Lefty and he calls me Hop-a-long. When Logan was telling me about this mission, yeah, to me it's a mission, to save the village, he said we were blood brothers. All of us in here are blood brothers. When we fight, we fight together and if we die, we die together. There won't be any officer a hundred miles away telling us what we can or can't do, who we can save or who to leave." He raised his fist, turned, and walked away from the table.

A few men clapped, then more, and then the entire room. Tears could be seen rolling down the cheeks of warriors.

Chapter Seven

The next day Special Agent Cosworth took his glasses off, laying them on his desk as the field agent walked into his office. He was still brooding and dark shadows surrounded his eyes, almost like a mask. His face was a pasty white. "What do you have, Arnie?"

"Donavan was picked up by someone in a black Chevy Tahoe. The license plates had mud on them so the security cameras couldn't get a number. We did check the train and bus stations and the airport. We think we've got something."

"Before you tell me, we're getting interference by someone with political connections, so don't discuss this with anyone other than me for the present time."

Field agent Arnie Spurlock nodded as he looked around the room. "Are you okay, boss?"

"Yeah, just talk to me, Arnie. Give me something, " Cosworth said, popping three Tums into his mouth.

"A private business jet owned by the World Broadcast Company took off from the airport approximately an hour after Donavan was picked up at the prison. Since it's private there wasn't a passenger manifest, but it landed at Newark International Airport."

"WBC is owned by one of the wealthier men in America. See if you can find out if WBC had any business in Lewisburg. I'm betting you won't. That's how Donavan left, I know it, but what's the connection?"

Cosworth said. "Too coincidental. You know what to do, check the taxies at the Newark airport, buses, limos, show his picture around and check their cameras. We might have something here, Arnie."

"I'll let you know if we come up with anything," Spurlock said. He left the office wondering if the old man was getting a little paranoid on that Donavan guy. Hell, the C.I. had been a scum-bag, and when he was killed it helped society. If Donavan did it or had it done, he should have gotten a medal, instead of prison. But, FBI agents shouldn't think that way, especially one of Cosworth's boys. Straight line, the law's the law. No in-between.

* * *

Finding the taxi that took Donavan to the hotel only took a day. Victor Ramos nodded his head when he saw the picture . "Si, Si, he called from the private concourse to be picked up. I take him over to New York City. To, uh, to, uh.... Sheet, I don't remember, now. You have to call dispatch and have them look on my records. Sorry, man."

After getting a warrant for the records from the taxi office, Agent Spurlock saw Ramos had dropped Donavan at the Empire Apartment Hotel on the corner of 18th and Highland, in Manhattan, where the sidewalks were filled with people all hours of the day and the streets overflowed with traffic.. The Empire was expensive, but not gaudy. Comfortable would describe it. There was a lobby with sofas and chairs, a manned front desk and a concierge in a glass office to the side.

When Spurlock showed his badge and asked if Shelby Donavan had rented an apartment from them, the desk clerk said he couldn't divulge the information.

After being told a warrant would be secured and the clerk shouldn't even think of breaking the smallest law, the clerk decided it wouldn't hurt to check the computer for the feds.

"No," he said. "No Shelby Donavan, no one with a last or first name of Donavan is staying here." Looking at Spurlock he said, turning the monitor, "Honest to God. You look."

"How about the World Broadcasting Company?"

"Just a second. Yes. They lease an apartment. Number 824." The clerk asked if there was anything else he could do for them.

Spurlock laid a picture of Donavan on the counter. "Have you seen this man?"

"Yeah. I think he started coming in about two or three days ago. This who you're looking for?"

"You are a bright one. One thing more," Spurlock said, leaning towards the young man reading his name tag pinned to his coat lapel. "Silas Underwood. Well Silas, I'll take it as a personal favor if you would keep this to yourself. We might be in and out for a few days and really don't want to have everyone in town know it. Kapish?"

"You bet, Agent." Underwood drew a finger across his mouth. "My lips are sealed."

"They better stay that way." Spurlock folded the picture, put it in his jacket pocket and turned to an agent, Jess Fuller, behind him. "Grab a seat and watch for him. I'll get Carson in here too, and have you guys relieved every six hours. Take turns if one of you have to hit the head. The van will be ready, so when you see him leave, call."

* * *

Shelby had come out of the elevator when he saw the two agents in the lobby, one of them questioning the desk clerk, holding a photograph in his hand. He didn't know if they were cops or possibly Logan left his men there, but they looked like feds to him. Both were clean cut with short hair, dark suits, bulges on their hips. Turning around he slipped back into the elevator and rode back up to the ninth floor, getting off, walking down the stairs to the eight floor and entering his apartment.

Logan answered the cell phone on the second ring. "What's up?"

"Did you pull your security men?"

"I told you I would, and I did. Yesterday. What's the problem?" Logan asked. He could hear the change in Shelby's voice. A little strained, a bit of excitement creeping out.

"There's two men in the lobby; one has a picture and is questioning the desk clerk. I think the FBI is looking for me. Probably that goddamn Cosworth finding out I was released and wants to haul my ass back to prison."

"Let me see what I can find out, Shelby. I think you better sneak out and find another place no one knows about, not even me."

"My thoughts exactly. Can you get me a passport under another name?"

"Shouldn't be a problem." A pause and then Logan said, "I'll get you lined up and you can work out the details with the guy. He's safe, we've used him before."

"I might have to meet you at the party rather than you giving me a lift," Shelby said. "I don't want to stay on the air too long. Call you later." He pushed the 'end' button and flipped the phone shut.

He wasn't sure how to get out of the building without being seen, or, should he just walk out like he doesn't suspect anything? If they were at the hotel to arrest him, he thought the feds would have already come to the apartment. Which meant they were putting him under surveillance. There was a slight adrenalin rush which excited him. Not a battle, but a damn good game afoot. He wondered if that was a sign of going a little psycho. Maybe, maybe not. No big deal.

The hallway was empty when he stepped out of the apartment. Closing the door, he plucked a piece of hair from his head, licked his fingers and ran them down the hair, then stuck one end a few inches from the bottom of the door, and the other end to the door molding. Anyone coming in would separate the hair from either the door or the molding showing that someone had entered his apartment. Shelby pulled his jacket and baseball cap on while he walked to the stairs at the end of the hall and trotted down to the main floor.

He wore a money belt with four-thousand dollars tucked inside - money Logan had left him in the briefcase. If his apartment was entered and searched, he didn't want the cash found which would probably add more suspicion to whatever the feds thought he was doing. He walked through the lobby and to the main door without looking at the two men sitting in chairs reading papers. Just for the hell of it, he pulled his cell phone out of his pocket, looked at the phone as if it were ringing, then put it to his ear and said, "Yes, Mr. President. I'm on my way sir." Shelby closed the phone, put it in his pocket and left the hotel, walking down 18th street, whistling.

"Did you hear what he said?" Fuller asked Carson, who nodded. "We better let Spurlock figure that one out. I don't want to say I think he might have received a call from the president of the country. I'd get fired. Let's go." They stood up and separated, Fuller leaving first and then Carson. They took up positions behind Donavan and began following him.

Carson called the van and two men exited, one carrying a leather case. They went into the hotel, took the elevator to the eight floor, picked the electronic lock on room 824 with a digital enumerating scanner, and went inside. The case contained five mini-wireless microphones and one wireless camera. One man installed the camera in an artificial plant on a side table near the flat screen TV. The other man hid the microphones in the living room, kitchen, both bedrooms, and the master bathroom, saying, "I hope this guy doesn't have bowel problems."

They were in the apartment twelve minutes and back in the van four minutes later. "Now comes the most boring part of the job," one agent said, settling into the seat in front of the control panel, checking the camera output and wireless strength of the microphones. "Everything is A-OK," he stated to his partner.

* * *

Shelby walked at a leisurely pace down the sidewalk, looking in store windows, apparently no destination in mind. After a half an hour, he came to the 33rd Street and Lexington IRT subway station, sliding into a mass of people all turning down into the subway entrance. He disappeared from the sight of Fuller and Carson. The two FBI agents looked at each other and started trotting towards the entrance.

Shelby walked down two levels, dropped a token through a slot and moved through the turnstile, going toward the subway trains. He suddenly moved quickly to the exit lanes and mixed in with a crowd of people leaving a train and heading to the stairway exits.

Putting on a pair of sunglasses, pitching his cap, and hunching over, he passed by the agents scouring the people getting on the subway.

Carson put his cell phone to his ear and said, "We think he boarded the northbound Lexington subway. We're getting on to try and find him. I'll get back to you at the first stop."

Glimpsing behind him, Shelby didn't see the agents coming out of the station. He walked down Parkway stopping in front of a two story brick building. Still not seeing the agents, he looked in the store front window of The Broadway Show Store for a few moments, and then entered the main door. Fifteen minutes later he came out of the store and whistled at a taxi driving down the street. Getting in, he gave the address of the Empire Apartment Hotel.

* * *

Fuller and Carson walked through all the cars without seeing Donavan. "I think he gave us the slip," Carson said. "Let's get off at the next stop and get back to the hotel."

Fuller nodded his head and cursed. "Dammit, I can't believe he spotted us. Maybe we just missed him somehow."

"Yeah, sure, Jess. No sweat, though. The surveillance guys will hear him when he gets to his apartment. " Carson chuckled. "I almost feel sorry for him thinking he got away from us."

* * *

The man had long gray hair that hung down over his collar, a gray mustache and goatee, and a large nose with a mole on the side. He wore a dark overcoat and walked into the Empire Apartment Hotel, going straight to the elevators. On the eighth floor, standing in front of room number 824, he bent down and didn't see the hair connected to the door and molding. Turning around, he went back to the elevator pushing the lobby button.

Fuller and Carson stepped off the subway at the first stop. They had requested a NYC PD patrolman take them to the Empire Apartment Hotel. "Lights and siren?" the patrolman had asked.

"No, just get us there safe and fast," Carson had answered the patrolman. Across the street from the hotel they entered the surveillance van. Inside the van he asked if there had been any activity in the room.

"Nope, quiet as a mortuary," the agent said. "Not even a knock on the door."

"Let's go in and wait, Jess. I'm betting he'll show, sooner or later," Carson said, opening the van door and getting out. Fuller followed him. They went inside the hotel and went to the desk. The desk clerk, Silas Underwood, was still on duty.

"Have you seen him?" Carson asked.

"No sir, not since he left earlier, when you were still here."

"Let's get comfortable, Jess. Might be a long day." Carson sat in an overstuffed leather chair facing the desk. Fuller took one of the couches. They casually glanced at the long-haired, big nosed, mustached-goateed man walking out of the lobby to the street. "How would you like to have a nose like that?" Fuller said. "I'd cut that mole off if it were me."

Shelby turned east and hailed a cab a block down. Man, he thought, it was interesting what kind of a face a guy could get at a theatre costume and makeup store. Five stars to The Broadway Show Store.

Chapter Eight

"Shelby called me and says he's being followed," Logan said as he walked into Jean Paul's office. "They were waiting at the hotel." He went on to tell how Shelby lost them at the subway station, went back to the hotel, found his apartment had been entered, so had left without going in. He was going to find another place. "He wants to make some different plans on meeting up with us."

"How could they have found him? And why?" Jean Paul asked.

"Shelby thinks it's the FBI agent who was in command when he was arrested in Texas. The agent's name is Cosworth. Apparently he's the special agent in charge for this area. The only thing Shelby can think of is Cosworth is pissed about him being released from prison, so he's out to arrest him for something."

Jean Paul went to the window and looked out. "I'm beginning to wonder if I've made a mistake with this." Turning back to face Logan, he asked, "What do you think?"

"All right. Here's the truth. If I were in your position and had your money, having my family face the Janjaweed coming, and knowing they are going to kill whoever they can, rape women and boys, destroy the village, you can bet your life I'd do what you're doing. And, Jean Paul, that's what you're doing. Betting your life, maybe even your freedom. But remember, no one is being forced to go over there, they want to, even though everyone of them knows he might not come back. We want to inherently stick up for the underdog, you can say that's what Americans have done for centuries. This isn't the government being a policeman to the world depending on what a country can do for us, this is someone not going to accept bullshit politics. So there's my honest take on it."

"And now," Jean Paul said with a sigh, "the FBI might be getting involved." Logan watched as Jean Paul walked back to his desk and sat down. "When you talk to Shelby, tell him—" He stopped at the sound of the satellite phone on his desktop ringing.

* * *

"This is preposterous!" Robert rose from his chair in Philip Reynolds' office. He had just been told by Reynolds that he wouldn't be in charge when Jean Paul took his leave of absence. "I'm going to talk to my brother and get this straightened out." Robert stormed out of the office, slamming the door behind him.

He tapped the toe of his shoe impatiently after poking the elevator button. When the door opened his finger stabbed the 54th floor button three times. His jaw ached from gritting his teeth on the ride up, thinking how he was being disrespected. When the elevator stopped on his floor, he had all intents of throwing Jean Paul's office door open and demanding to be appointed the interim CEO, instead of Reynolds.

The walk to the office calmed him down a bit. Instead of throwing the office door open, he eased it open just as Jean Paul mentioned the FBI might be getting involved and starting to say something about someone named Shelby when Jean Paul's satellite phone rang. Robert stepped back and silently closed the door, then quickly walked back down the hall to the elevator.

* * *

Logan noticed the door knob on the office door turning. He walked over and opened the door a few inches and saw the receding back of Robert. He wondered what the hell Robert was doing there and what had the brother heard, if anything.

Jean Paul ended the call. "That was Aafreen, asking when we would be arriving. The villagers that aren't fighting have left, taking the livestock. They're getting quite anxious waiting for us, afraid they'll be attacked soon. She did say some men are keeping watch several miles from the village though they estimate the Janjaweed should be within twenty miles by the end of the week. What are you doing at the door?"

"Just checking to make sure our conversation is private." Logan sat down in the chair next to Jean Paul's. "I can get everyone ready to leave in five days. The passports and WBC ID's will be done by tomorrow. Shelby should know when the weapons and gear will be in the country, if they aren't already. We'll coordinate getting men there after the equipment's been delivered to Darfur. Once we land, load the bus, and cross the border, there shouldn't be a problem until we engage the Janjaweed."

"My station chief in Chad says the Central African Republic isn't stable," Jean Paul said. "How about your contact? Can he help us?"

"He's handing out bribes left and right. Both government and rebel forces, so we should be able to cross the border without any interference. You're spending a lot of cash, but this is our best route to take." Logan glanced at the door again.

"I agree. Do whatever it takes to get us to Kumkjeri."

* * *

Shelby called Sam and asked if she could pick him up at Antonio's Lounge, on 42nd and Dexter in an hour. He told the cab driver to drop him off a few blocks east of the lounge. From there he walked to Antonio's and took a booth inside. There was a lunch buffet to the side and the smells nearly made his mouth water. After ordering an ice tea with a shot of vodka, he went to the buffet and filled two plates with Italian food. Back at the table he began eating when his cell phone vibrated in his pocket.

"You've got me," he answered.

"We think you should go over as soon as possible. Our group is leaving in four days from tomorrow on a chartered jet."

"No problem, tell me where to get the paperwork and I'll head out tomorrow. The merchandise will be delivered day after tomorrow and just waiting for me to take possession. You sound a little edgy," Shelby said. "Getting too old for this kind of action, my friend?"

"Hell no. A little while ago, in a meeting, I think the brother heard some info with your name mentioned. I'm not sure, but there could be problems. He's pissed about not getting promoted. Man, I hate talking over these things and not sure of the security." Logan said.

"If the phones weren't good, then every crook and politician would be in jail. What about the brother? Is he a risk to the operation?"

Shelby saw Samantha walk into the lounge and look around. She looked past him and started scowling. He told Logan to hold on, got up and walked over to her. "Hey baby, how about a good time?"

"Piss off, slick," she said, turning away from him.

"Sam, it's me."

She turned back to him, ran her hand up his face, and said, "Good Lord, Shelby, you don't look anything at all like you."

He led her to the booth, told her to grab some food and he'd be finished with his call in a minute. She nodded and went to the steam tables.

"Sorry about that. Do you want me to take care of the problem?"

"God no, Shelby! He's Jean Paul's brother!"

"I'm not talking about whacking him. Christ, you must think I'm one hell of a criminal," Shelby said.

"Who were you talking to?"

"A trustworthy friend. What are you going to do about the brother," Shelby said. "Especially since you said you're not sure what he heard, if anything."

"I've got to think about it, probably talk to Jean Paul. You don't need to worry, just be careful." Logan told Shelby how to contact the man for his passport and other identification, and he would have some more cash left there for him. "Where are you going to fly out of?"

"To be on the sly side, I'm not going to mention the place on the phone. No offense, partner. That might keep the feds from getting in my face. I'll see you on the other side of the border, as the Mexicans say." Donavan pushed the "End" button and flipped the phone closed.

After he finished his call, Sam sat down and began eating. "Everything okay?" she asked between bites.

Shelby told her about the feds and probably some kind of surveillance in his room, how he avoided them in the hotel and could he stay with her tonight?

"I believe this is the first time you've ever thrown a request to sleep with me alongside your narration of the day you had," she said through a mouthful of food.

"I'm trying make up for lost time since I got out of the pen. How about it?"

51

"Hmmm, okay. Daddy says to tell you the merchandise is leaving the Republic tomorrow. You'll have three days to take possession." She picked a napkin up and dabbed at her lips. "I'm going to go with you."

"Oh no, it's going to be too damn dangerous. Why would you even think of going?"

"Simple, Shelby. I don't know how much time we'll have together, so I'm taking advantage. You forget I can shoot any type of rifle and pistol, so I'll be an asset to you and your guys. No use arguing. If you try to ditch me or keep me from going, I'll have daddy renege on the deal. He can get the stuff out the country as easy as he's getting it in. You'll probably lose your man's money, he'll be pissed and have you killed. Sounds like there aren't too many choices."

Shelby closed his eyes and frowned, deep in thought. Then he smiled, took the fork out of her hand and said, "I have a couple of things to do tonight, then we'll leave day after tomorrow. Do you have a passport?"

She nodded her head. "What are we doing tonight? I'm asking because I'll be tagging along."

"Documents, money, get plane reservations. It will take us close to twenty hours with good flight connections. Let's go to your place and I'll start making our reservations."

* * *

After what seemed like an eternity on the phone, Shelby dropped the phone in its cradle. He checked his watch, stood up, paced around the large living room of Sam's apartment, and stopped in front of the fireplace, holding his hands out to the warmth of the gas logs.

"I'm having one hell of a time with the plane connections," he said. "I'm going to make one more call then we need to leave. The passport guy won't wait if we're late."

The call was to Logan. After telling him about the time delays getting to the Central African Republic on commercial airlines, Shelby asked if a long range business jet could be charted for him. He told Logan he wanted to fly out of Toronto, and would tell the pilots the flight plan when the jet rental was confirmed. He also told Logan he needed one more WBC identification, and he'd fill in the name and get a picture for it.

"Who's it for?"

"My partner, don't worry about it," Shelby said.

"Okay, okay. I'll get on hiring the jet and get back to you, inside of an hour if I'm lucky, " Logan said. He told Shelby there would be a secure satellite phone waiting for him and the additional WBC identification when he had his ID and passport made. "You should get to Toronto as soon as you can. Since the flight will be international, go to Pearson International Airport."

"Gotcha. Here's hoping we're being overly cautious, but better cautious than seeing the feds grab me," Shelby said. "Once we get over to Darfur, there's no turning back. We'll be like William Wallace, and kick ass. Now get off the damn phone, Logan, you have a lot of work to do."

Chapter Nine

Robert Allahamba entered his brother's office taking the chair Jean Paul pointed to in front of the desk. He glanced at Logan, who sat in a chair at the side of the desk..

"You had a confrontation with Phillip yesterday. About he being the interim CEO while I'm gone. Is that correct?" Jean Paul asked. His voice had a sharp edge to it and his eyes held Robert, who nodded solemnly. "All right. Tell me why you should have been appointed instead of Phillip, and we'll talk about it."

"I'm your brother, I should be the acting CEO. You haven't me given any responsibility since I've been here. Don't you think being in charge of building maintenance contracts is a company joke? Demeaning?" Robert crossed his arms and frowned. "I came over here for you. To help you out, be a confidant, be someone you could feel secure in eventually assisting you in running the company."

"That's quite admirable, and I appreciate it. Perhaps I haven't been as supportive as I should have been. I'm sorry if that's the case," Jean Paul said. He looked at Logan for a moment.

The intercom beeped. "Mr. Allahamba, Special Agent Miller on line two," his secretary said.

"Thank you, Louise." He picked up the phone and poked a button. "Agent Miller, what can I do for you?" Jean Paul nodded a few times then said, "Max Nueman is in my investment department and I believe he's used insider information for his personal gain. If you contact

Ross Bellings, at extension 3375, he'll give you the information. Yes, thank you sir, I appreciate it." Jean Paul hung the phone up. "It's hard to trust anyone when they're in the position to take advantage of you. Remember that, Robert."

"You called the FBI on this guy?" Robert asked.

"Of course, we can't have our reputation tarnished."

"Sure, sure. I agree," Robert said.

Jean Paul took a folder out a desk drawer, opened it, scanned some papers, then said to Robert, "You've had some valid points on me not promoting you. Experience is the main reason and I am guilty of not giving you that experience. Here's what I'm willing to do."

Jean Paul told him he would assign him to his five major stations: Los Angeles, Seattle, Boston, Dallas and finally New York City. Robert would work with the station chief for three months at each location to see how each location has to meet different criteria for the viewers.

"This is an opportunity for you Robert. If you want to advance in the company, you'll fly out tomorrow on the company jet to L.A. We have a company apartment that's quite comfortable you can stay in." He paused for a moment. "So, do you want to accept this route of promotion?"

Even a blind man could have seen the light turn on in Robert's face. He smiled, showing white teeth bleached from an expensive dentist. "Of course I'll do it, Jean Paul. Thank you, thank you so much. I won't let you down."

"You need to go pack, so take the rest of the afternoon off. Louise has the paperwork you'll need. Don't let this opportunity slip away from you, Robert. We're on a slippery slope, you and I."

Robert bounded out of his chair, shook hands with Logan, then hugged Jean Paul. "I won't let you down, I swear. This is all I wanted, a chance, brother. Thank you." He radiated an energy Jean Paul had never seen before.

Robert walked to the office door, opened it, then turned to Jean Paul and Logan and said, "God be with you." He closed the door behind him as he left.

"This might actually be a benefit for both of us, you know it, Logan? Rather than just getting him out of our hair, he could possibly turn into an asset to the company," Jean Paul said, a small smile creeping across his face. "The little act on the phone was quite the idea, my friend."

"Thanks. Back to business. We're ready to board tomorrow afternoon. Since it's such a long trip, and we'll be flying all night, the guys should be able to get some sleep. You ready for this?"

"If you remember, Shelby told me to watch a movie Donovan mentioned. I did, last night. After it ended, I almost cancelled the mission, wondering if I was on a fool's errand. If we can defeat the Janjaweed... not just defeat, decimate them, and my money can get enough pressure exerted to not let this happen again to defenseless villagers, then it's worth it. So to answer your question. Damn right, I'm ready."

* * *

The next night, Samantha, with Shelby in the passenger seat, pulled her car into a space of a busy parking garage on 128th in Brooklyn. They left the car and walked four blocks down a dark street of closed shops, finally knocking on the door of a tailor shop, with a weak light shining from inside the store. They were ushered in by a short, portly man with receding gray hair, and thick glasses. "Everything is paid for and I have a package for you," he said, never giving his name.

They went into the back of the shop, where Shelby, his hair, newly dyed a dark brown, a matching mustache with goatee, and looking out of clear, black framed, horn-rimmed glasses, sat down in front of a camera. Under a high intensity lamp, sat two identification cards, and one blank passport. The cobbler, as document forgers were called, took Shelby's picture, filled in the information data, applied several stamps from countries entered and exited, then had him sign the new passport and WBC identification. For Samantha, her picture was taken and used to make her WBC identification card. After an hour, they left, walked back to the parking garage, getting in the car and left.

"Tony Burma. I don't think I like that as much as Shelby Donavan," Sam said, as she drove towards Queens, and LaGuardia Airport.

"Tony Burma and Sam Pershing. Sounds pretty audacious to me," Shelby replied. "Makes us sound like a couple of Ian Fleming characters."

* * *

They parked in the public lot at the airport, hopped a terminal bus to Terminal 5, purchased two tickets on Air Canada Express to Pearson International Airport in Toronto, and left one hour later without any questions, side-way looks from security, or being handcuffed by an Authority policeman. Shelby said it was the luck of the Irish to catch a plane so soon.

Two hours and forty-five minutes later, they landed at Pearson International Airport. Going through customs was a breeze, then what took the most time was finding transportation to the private/small business airway terminal. Shelby finally hired a taxi to take them around the airport and drop them off at their terminal. Going inside, a sign pointed the way to Leisure Enterprises Jet service. At the desk, Shelby handed the attendant the papers Logan had sent with the WBC IDs. She in turn introduced the pilots and flight attendant to them.

A Gulfstream IVSP waited on the tarmac. After they entered the cabin, took seats and fastened their safety belts, the twin Rolls-Royce engines fired off. At 12:25 in the morning, the jet lifted off the runway, en route to Dakar, Senegal, Africa, where the jet would refuel and the passengers would be checked into the country through customs. Shelby and Sam each had a vodka tonic, a light meal, then reclined their leather seats back to take advantage of the darkness and sleep as much as possible.

* * *

After flying eight hours at a little over 500 mph, and a time difference of plus five hours, the Gulf Stream touched down at Lèopold Sèdar Senghor International Airport, Dakar, Senegal, Africa, a few minutes after 1:00 P.M. The jet taxied to a fuel station where the engines were shut down, the passengers and flight crew off loaded and escorted to customs check in. A tall, lanky black man began filling the jet's tanks with fuel. Armed soldiers patrolled the terminal in pairs, their Ak-47's slung on their backs. A bored customs clerk asked their business, which Shelby/Tony said was international news reporting for WBC and showed his work ID and passport. Sam showed her passport and work ID. The clerk's eyes moved up and down her body, stamped the documents then moving them along with a wave of his hand. Forty minutes they were airborne, heading to the last stop in the plane, Birao, Central African Republic.

* * *

At the Newark International Airport, a Boeing long range business jet took off and climbed into a sky laced with dark, cumulus clouds. Twenty men and one woman sat in the roomy cabin while two attendants walked the aisle taking orders for food and drink as the jet climbed to a cruising altitude of 37,500 feet.

The cabin was basically quiet with a few men talking softly to each other while the majority had earphones on and their eyes focused on the movie screen.

"My heart is beating twice as fast as usual," Jean Paul told Logan. They sat next to each other in the front of the cabin.

"It'll settle down. What we want to do now is relax, get your mind to enjoy the quiet and solitude."

"Is this how you felt before going on patrol, in Iraq?"

"Sure, every time. We wondered how we'd perform under fire, fight without getting killed, get back to the post at the end of the day. When someone began walking towards us without a weapon in sight, the first thought was, 'Is this guy a suicide bomber?' Shoot him, or her, or wait and see how they would act as they got closer," Logan said. His head was tilted back and eyes closed.

"So what did you do?"

Logan opened his eyes and turned to him. "Sometimes killed them, sometimes not. Every instance was different. You're going to do fine, Jean Paul."

"Thank you, Logan." He turned and looked over his seat down the aisle. "I think we have some good men."

And then he thought, my God, to say killing someone so easily, no remorse, another day another couple of men to kill.

"I do too, though who knows, there might be one or two psychopaths, a couple of druggies... things we'll find out when it's the most inconvenient."

Four hours into the flight, dinner was served, lights dimmed and the drone of the jet comforted several men and one woman who's thoughts flashed and sparkled with energy and fear.

Chapter Ten

SAC Cosworth called Spurlock into his office. "Give me an update on Donavan, Arnie."

"We still haven't found him. All the airports are being checked and so far, nothing. We did find one interesting thing, though. This afternoon a jet chartered by the World Broadcasting Company took off from NIA."

"Flight plan to...?" Cosworth took a bottle of Tums off his desk, shook four into his hand and plopped them in his mouth.

"Dakar, Africa."

"See if someone can contact the company and find out why the plane is going and who's on it. Tell them it has to do with international terrorism. If they're good Americans, they should tell us."

"Okay, anything else?" Spurlock had his notebook out, pen in hand.

"Dammit, do I have to think of everything? See if there's a way to check all the international airports in a three or four hundred mile area for any chartered flights to Dakar. If Donavan has left the country, my nose is telling me he's either on the jet that left or he's leaving on another one somewhere. Now, get on it." His hand went to his chest. "Goddamn heartburn."

"Maybe you should see a doctor about that, sir. You don't seem to be feeling well," Spurlock said.

"Since you're not a doctor but an FBI agent, I don't believe you need to be giving out a diagnosis,"

Cosworth said. "Now anything else relative to the orders I just gave you?"

"I'm not sure if we can get the Canadian airports to be cooperative. After we held the Canadian a couple weeks and interrogated him, the government up there didn't buy we thought he was involved with Al-Qaida. Which of course, he wasn't," Spurlock said. He put a hand over his mouth to prevent the Special Agent in Charge seeing the smile cracking across his face.

"Granted, I made a mistake with that particular incident. No one is perfect. He lost a couple of weeks and I lost a promotion, so I would say we're even. Wouldn't you?" Cosworth said.

"Oh, definitely, sir. I'll get busy on this unless you have something else for me."

"Leave, find me Donavan."

After Spurlock closed the door as he left, Cosworth dialed a number on his phone.

"Central Intelligence Agency," the voice answered.

Chapter Eleven

The co-pilot sat down in a seat across from Shelby and Sam, a sheet of paper in his hand. "We've just been advised by the company to have you leave the plane as soon as we land. There's reported fighting between rebels and the army within a few miles of the airport. We can't take a chance of being fired on or stranded there if the one runway for a jet would be blown to hell. We land in fifteen minutes."

"Give me your satellite phone, Shelby," Samantha said. She took it and poked numbers in as she walked to the back of the plane. A few moments later she could be heard speaking.

"Can we get our gear out from the cabin?" Shelby asked. The co-pilot, whose name was Henry Jeffers, nodded and with Shelby, walked toward the back while passing Sam coming back up the aisle. Jeffers opened a door at the rear bulkhead, stepped in and handed Shelby their duffle bags.

They stuffed the bags into two seats next to the cabin loading door, strapping the seat belts around them. Jeffers went back to the cockpit and Shelby dropped into his seat.

"What's with the call?" he asked, taking the phone back.

"Calling the Ukrainian in charge of the guys who brought the equipment over. His name's Petro Doyzhenko. Daddy uses him for most of the business transactions because of his connections and experience. I've met and worked with him on several deals, he's honorable and more importantly, dependable. He's been waiting for us in Birao," Sam said.

"Sounds like you might have shared a bit more than work, my sweet."

"Stuff it, slick," she said, slugging him on the shoulder. "We are good friends, but nothing more since you got out of the pen."

"I haven't been out a week, yet!"

She grinned and blew him a kiss.

The flight attendant came back and told them landing would be sooner than originally thought, the pilots were going in for what was called a hot landing. Five minutes before touchdown and they should be sure their seat belts were on and tight. The sound of the engines powering back could be heard and felt in the cabin.

After the attendant left, Sam continued, "Petro's meeting us at the airport and will take us to the vehicles and equipment, about a hundred and twenty miles or so inside Darfur." The plane made a sharp left turn while quickly descending. "Holy hell, grab my hand, Shelby." She reached out and squeezed his hand so tight he yelped.

The jet came in fast, hit the runway and nose-dived when the pilot pushed the brakes hard. It took them to the end of the strip to get stopped. As the jet turned around, engines still running for a fast take off, Sam pointed at the window at the same time the captain said over the cabin speaker, "Three minutes to get off before we get the hell out of here. We've been informed the rebels are breaching the airport." Even with the training for being calm in the face of fire, the pilot sounded tense.

Sam said Petro was heading towards them in a car, his hand waving out the window, so they needed to grab their bags on the way out. The flight attendant ran to the back, opened the door and lowered the steps at the same time the car, an older Ford station wagon, slammed on its brakes and came to a screeching stop near the ladder. The bags dropped to the ground near the station wagon.

A man in his mid-thirties, dark hair and wearing sunglasses, bounded out of the car shouting, "Samantha, come on, there's no time." He ran to the ladder and took her from the last rung. Shelby had a hold of the hand rails and slid down behind her. Automatic gunfire and mortar blasts could be heard. Smoke drifted towards them from the far buildings in the airport.

Sam grabbed both bags, gave them to Petro, who opened the back tailgate and threw them into the rear of the Ford. After Sam climbed into the front seat, Shelby hopped in the back seat. Petro yanked the car into gear and spun the front tires as it took off. They raced through an open gate leaving the airport when the chartered jet flew over their heads and banked to the right.

"Holy shit!" Shelby yelled when the jet exploded, the smoke trail from a rocket still sharp in the sky. The main fuselage of the Gulf Stream spiraled to the ground, engulfed in flames. Black smoke rolled off the tarmac engulfing the car until it turned down a street flanked by warehouses. "I've got to warn Logan." He pulled the sat phone from his pocket and furiously poked the numbers in.

Logan answered on the second ring. Shelby told him to abort from landing at the airport because of the firefight. "Hold on a sec," Logan told him. A pause, and then, "Okay, our pilots know. Where should we land? Our ETA is 2: 00 A.M. on our current course. "

"Standby." Shelby said, "You have any idea where we should land the other jet with our troops? I can't think of any place within five hundred miles other than Birao." The windows were open blowing hot air into the car. Sweat ran down their faces.

"How big of a plane?" Petro asked, turning onto a side street heading away from the airport and the fighting.

"I'd say a small airliner size, there's twenty-one guys and their gear. It'll take a long runway," Shelby said. "What kind of jet, Logan?"

"Boeing 737."

"737. What do you think?"

"There's an abandoned military airport 150 miles from here. That's where we landed with your equipment. Closer to the village than here."

"What kind of plane?"

"C-130. A little rough landing, but no problems. They shouldn't have any," Petro answered.

"Logan, there's an abandoned airport 150 miles from here where a loaded C-130 landed. Our man says you shouldn't have a problem landing there. I'm going to give him the phone and he can give you the coordinates." Shelby handed the phone to Petro.

He rattled off some longitude and latitude numbers before saying, "There's no lights. We'll have to use the vehicle lights and the landing lights to get you down. No, no obstructions. I don't believe you will experience much difficulty." Petro listened for a minute and then said,

"Are you crazy? Because of customs. We don't use them when we fly weapons and the like into a country." He handed the phone back to Shelby.

"We'll try it," Logan told him. "I'll call when we're thirty minutes from touchdown--- Later." The phone went dead with a click.

Petro turned again and gave the car the gas as they shot down a narrow street. Two blocks down from them at an intersection, a group of men came into the street, their hands up and waving. Behind them a truck pulled into the middle of the street, blocking it off.

"They've got guns, hold on!" The Ford went into a controlled slide. Petro pulled the emergency brake handle hard, which brought the tail end of the car around, so when the gas pedal was slammed to the floor, the car took off in the direction they'd just come from, tires burning. Behind, the men vaulted into the truck, some started shooting automatic rifles at them.

"Get down," Petro yelled. Bullets blew out the back window, narrowly missing Samantha. Another turn to the right, down one block and another turn to the right had them going parallel to the direction they had been traveling before meeting the rebels. Near an alley, he slid the car to a stop, jumped out and peeked down the alley. A moment later, he saw the truck fly past on the other side of the block, in the wrong direction. Running back to the car, his thumb was held in the air. "Let's get the hell out of here," he said, pulling back into the street.

"Samantha, under the rear compartment rug are three pistols with some extra magazines. Get them out for us, will you?"

She leaned over, rummaged around and brought three Glock 23's to her seat. Handing one to Shelby, another to Petro, the third pistol went into the band of her pants. She reached over to the back again and had six magazines in her hands. "Here you go, boys," Sam said, dropping four over to the front seat. Checking to make sure her Glock had one in the chamber and a magazine full of bullets, she told Petro, "I'm smelling gas. The tank must have been hit. You better stop and we'll check it."

Several bullet holes were scattered on the back of the Ford. Underneath a small drip of gasoline pooled on the street.

"Great. What's next?" Shelby said. He crawled under the rear bumper. "I see the hole, got a rag or something?"

Petro took a bandana from his neck, laying it in Shelby's outstretched hand. Shelby twisted it into a tight roll and then stuffed half of the bandana into the hole of the gas tank. "The leak's slowed down, but I don't know for how long," Shelby said, crawling out from under the car.

When they drove down the street, Petro said they would have to find another car to steal.

"You mean this one is stolen?" Shelby asked.

"Yeah, easier than buying one, and what the hell, everyone does it around here," Petro told him. He called someone on his cell phone and told the person to start heading towards the city to meet them. "Samantha, there's an AK-47 under the back seat, be a dear and bring it out with the extra ammo, if you will," he said after finishing the call. "Nothing to worry about, we'll find—"

Bursts of gunfire raked over the car. "Oh, shit," Petro yelled, flooring the gas pedal. Behind them were the rebels in the truck. At least three leaning over the cab roof, firing automatic rifles.

"Hang on." Petro skidded around a corner. When the car straightened, Shelby jumped into the back seat and took the rifle from Samantha.

When the rebel's truck turned behind them, he opened fire, shooting through the rear window, shattering what remained of it. Shelby emptied his magazine and saw one man who had been firing from the cab roof fall out of sight. "Got one, I think. Good thing these guys are piss poor shots."

Suddenly the car started shuddering and the engine quit. They coasted to the curb near an old cluster of abandoned buildings.

"Come on, hurry," Petro yelled, running into the second building. They scrambled up a staircase, bolted down a hallway and entered a deserted apartment.

The truck's brakes squealed as it came to a stop in front of the buildings. Five men climbed out, all carrying automatic rifles. The leader motioned with his arm towards the building Petro and the others had gone into.

Shelby kneeled by the door, his head barely sticking out. "They're coming," he whispered.

Chapter Twelve

The rebels searched through the ground floor rooms before climbing the stairs. The leader pointed to two men and motioned them to go into the first apartment. The other two checked the next one. "No one," both pairs said, coming back into the hallway.

The leader, whose name was Kaseeb, stood tall, showed bad teeth when he spoke, and had burn scars over his bare arms. "Throw your weapons into the hall, then come out with your hands raised very, very high. You have nowhere to hide, or go. We won't harm you, I promise." At this, Kaseeb smiled along with the others. There was no argument or orders given. When the whites came out with hands in the air, they would be gunned down.

Shelby still had the AK-47. He leaned back and in a low voice said, "We're in deep shit. Here's what I think we oughta do," he said, then whispered to Petro and Sam.

"Don't shoot, we're coming out," Shelby yelled. A pistol flew out of the room and clattered on the hallway floor. "That's the only gun we have." Petro, Samantha and Shelby stepped into the hallway and cut loose. Shelby had the AK on automatic and sprayed the rebels with bullets, Petro and Samantha fired as fast as they could pull the Glocks' triggers.

The top of Kaseeb's head blew off in a spray of blood and bone. The other four tried firing back but screamed as they were hit by the gunfire. One tried running back down the stairs and damned near made it until Petro leaned over the railing and put two .40 caliber rounds in his back. The gunfight took less than a minute. Four men were dead in the hallway, another at the bottom of the stairs.

With weapons raised and ready to fire at the first sight of a rebel, Shelby picked up the Glock on the floor, then the three crept down the stairs and out the door. No one waited and no shots were fired at them. "The car's had it, let's take the truck," Petro said. He climbed in the driver's side and started the truck while Sam sat down in the passenger side. Shelby told him to wait for a minute, heaved himself into the bed of the truck, grabbed the arm of the rebel he'd killed in the chase, and dragged the body to the back, then shoved it out. There was a mushy, soft plop as it hit the street, face down. Shelby jumped down and climbed in beside Sam. "Hit it, my man."

The truck took off in a lurch and clanked as Petro shifted gears. They drove down the street and only once saw what looked like rebels rushing a furniture store. Both Shelby and Petro pulled their shirts over their heads like head scarves, looking more like the rebels. After several turns the street straightened out heading west. Buildings were left behind and desert took their place.

"We have about twenty-five miles to make the border. Hopefully the soldiers will be in the city fighting instead of manning the gate," Petro said.

"Is it something we can blow through if they're there?" Shelby asked Petro, as he stroked the AK-47 next to him.

"I think so. It's just a few wooden planks nailed together next to a little guard hut. They turn a winch to lower it and raise it. Not modern at all. We all tend to forget how primitive this country is. Rebels fighting for Islam, soldiers fighting for the president. No one wins, just killing until one or the other retreats and whoever is left is the winner until another fight."

The truck could only max out at forty-five miles an hour. Nearly an hour later, the gate and hut came into sight. A long ditch ran along the border preventing anyone from going around, but there weren't any vehicles parked at the hut. As they pulled up to the lowered gate, one soldier who looked to be about sixteen years old, with weary eyes, came out and held his hand up.

"I'll handle this," Petro said. "Don't do or say anything." He stopped and leaned out the window. "Hiya," he said to the approaching guard. "We need to pass through to South Sudan."

The guard looked at the truck and gave Petro a once-over. "How many?"

"Three."

"Five hundred US dollars," he said, holding his hand out, palm up.

"Very reasonable," Petro said. He reached down, stuck his arm out of the window with the Glock in it, and pulled the trigger. The guard dropped straight down to the ground, twitched a bit, then was motionless.

"Jesus! What the hell did you do that for? I've got the money," Samantha said. She looked behind her and to the side, as if to see a platoon of soldiers running towards them. "He was just a boy."

Petro shoved the truck into gear, ran through the gate, shifted the gears and turned to Shelby and Sam. "If we'd have paid, he'd have either shot us or robbed us. These people have no honor, and don't kid yourself, Samantha, age means nothing."

The road quickly turned to gravel, then beaten down dirt and sand. In a few areas gravel had been thrown down, though the farther they traveled the less maintenance there was on the road until finally, none at all. The truck bounced and jerked as it hit holes and washouts. Going around a corner, the truck bottomed out on a rock sticking out of the dirt in a low depression. There was a loud scrap as Petro gave it the gas, lurching it out onto the level part of the road.

"Damn!" Petro said, pointing to a red light flickering on the dash. A moment later the engine died, with an odor of burnt oil. Smoke drifted up from under the hood. He climbed out and stuck his head under the front fender. Standing up, he pulled a finger across his throat. "We killed it. There's a hole in the oil pan and the shit is pouring out."

"What's the next move?" Shelby asked, getting down from the cab. He put his hand up to help Samantha down, but she ignored it and dropped to the ground. "You're welcome."

"Think nothing of it, Shelby. Thanks, but quit being the chivalrous Irishman. I can take care of myself." She walked to the back of the truck, kicking sand. "So, what are we going to do?"

"If you'll stop whining and listen, you'll see," Petro said. "Remember when I made the call after the car got shot up?" He nodded to the west. Coming low over the horizon was a transport helicopter, painted desert camouflage.

The copter circled and landed by the truck. Dust from the rotors blinded them for a few moments. "Your chariot," Petro yelled. He and Samantha made it to the helicopter and boarded, Shelby a couple steps behind. Petro slapped the pilot on the back, put headphones on and sat in the co-pilot's seat. He motioned for the other two to put the headphones on hanging behind them.

It took forty-five minutes for the Russian MI-8T to get to the abandoned airfield. Next to a dilapidated building were parked several transport trucks and military Jeep style vehicles. At the end of the runway, near the vehicles, the Lockheed C-130 dwarfed the building and vehicles.

"I'm impressed," Shelby said, as the helicopter hovered away from the C-130, then set down. The engine died and the rotors began slowing. They climbed out with the pilot and walked to the building. Inside about a dozen men drank coffee. Several waved at Petro when he entered.

He was asked if they were leaving that afternoon or early evening. "Tomorrow morning. We have to assist in the last plane coming." Petro told them of the battle in the city between the rebels and soldiers and the passenger jet landing at the airfield in the early morning. "About two-ish. We'll line the trucks up on both sides of the runway and have the 130 facing down the runway with its landing lights on. Once it's landed, we get ready to leave. Or I should say you will. I'm staying."

There was a murmur of voices. Shelby, standing next to Petro, raised his hands to quiet the men. "Anyone who wants to stay and help fight the Janjaweed with us will be handsomely paid and appreciated."

Heads were shaking no and one man stood up looking around at the seated men. He said, "We're merchants and transporters, not mercenaries." There was a general sound of agreement. "In the morning, after your jet lands, we will be flying out. Petro, we wish you would come with us."

"I probably should, Fredrick, but no. We will get together in Kiev after this is settled. I'll buy the beer with my pay." Laughter and some handshakes followed Petro as he left the building. A silence was heavy as the men looked at Shelby and Samantha.

"We'll be with Petro if any of you change your mind." He put a hand on Sam's elbow and guided her out. They caught up with Petro walking towards the C-130.

"Rest, then my men will position the trucks and plane before it gets dark."

"Petro, are you sure you want to join us?" Sam asked, her eyes questioning.

"Shelby, excuse us, please," Samantha asked. After Shelby nodded and gave them some distance, Petro said, "I see the way you look at him and he looks at you. Maybe there's a chance for me, maybe not, but what the hell, I've nothing to lose in trying. Right?"

"You might lose your life when the fighting starts," she replied.

"From Shelby or the Janjaweed?" A smile crossed his face.

* * *

The good: a full moon, no wind, no mountains anywhere close.

The bad: landing a twenty-five passenger jet on an abandoned World War II airstrip with no runway lights.

Logan sat in the jump seat of the pilot's cockpit with his cell phone to his ear. Ahead, near the horizon, dim lights shined parallel to each other. "We see the lights. Are they all on?" Brighter lights came on shining down the landing strip. He nodded then said to the pilots, "The landing lights are on the C-130, they're lighting flares at the end of the strip."

The pilot asked the length of the strip. "5800 feet," Logan answered.

"All right, everyone buckle up tight, here we go." The co-pilot lowered the flaps and the landing gear.

The jet shuttered and the engine noise became thunder. "Tell them I'm doing one low level fly-by."

The jet came in fifty feet off the ground at 225 knots just over the C-130. It stayed level to the end of the runway then banked left and made a long turn heading back in the direction of the C-130. Another turn and the jet was dropping down for its landing. They hit the ground at 140 knots with a bone-jarring jolt. The nose dove as the pilot and co-pilot shoved on the brake pedals and rudder controls. "Going too fast, full reverse thrust." The pilot said in a calm voice. The engines reversed and screamed as the plane shuddered violently. The few lights from the vehicles flew by.

"130....125....100....we're running out of runway," the co-pilot said. Logan swallowed hard, his hand clinched tight around his prosthetic one. "80....60....there's the end, we aren't going to make it," the co-pilot said.

* * *

Smoke rolled up from the tires as the brake pedals were shoved down as far as they would go. The jet shook and shuttered more as the pilots kept the brakes to the floor. The pilot alternated the rudder pedals, making the tail end of the jet slide from side to side. They ran off the end of the runway, still braking.

If God looked down on anyone, it was the occupants of the jet. After the runway ended, rough, but level sand and dirt, packed down hard from sun and rain, continued past the strip for another 400 yards. The jet finally stopped two hundred yards past the end of the runway. Logan wiped sweat off his face. "Oh, man, tell me we made it."

"We did," the pilot said, pulling his ear phones off. "We'll just have to start a little farther from the asphalt when we take off." He saw Logan's look. "No problem, Logan, trust me."

The jet taxied back to the building, where Shelby greeted the men as they climbed down the emergency steps. "Welcome to Darfur. Drinks and food are in the luxurious terminal." He stepped up to Logan and shook his hand. "I was wondering for a moment if you were going to be joining us in one piece, phony hand excepted."

"Yeah, me too. I think we better get the plane unloaded, get some rest then head for the village at first light. We estimate about three days before the Janjaweed will be in an attack position, though it could be sooner." They walked towards the building when Logan stopped and put a hand on Shelby's arm. "Who was the other ID for?"

"A dear friend and the daughter of the man who arranged all of the weapons and equipment for us. Her name's Samantha, a psychologist by trade who's been working with vets. Tough as nails, and," he looked around, "she and I are together, maybe something more in the future." A big smile stretched across his face. "I'll introduce her after we get the unloading done."

* * *

Logan's men unloaded their gear to the waiting trucks. He assigned two men to each vehicle telling them to get what rest they could because the unit would be leaving at dawn for the village. Shelby would be in the lead UAZ with a GPS. If everything went well, the men should arrive at the village in four to five hours. Logan, Jean Paul and Petro would take the helicopter with Lee Prescott piloting, after he took a check ride. They would check the route and a several mile radius around the village to make sure there wasn't an ambush or rebels waiting for them.

Shelby brought Sam to Logan and introduced her. "I've heard a lot of stories about you, Logan. It's nice to finally meet you, though I thought you were ten feet tall." She shook his right hand with a strong grip. "Is that correct? To shake your prosthetic?"

"Yeah. In fact, besides Shelby, you're the only person to have done that. Makes it feel less conspicuous. Thank you." Samantha and Logan visited for a few more minutes until she said they had better get some sleep.

Shelby winked at Logan as Sam and he headed towards the jet. Logan gave him a thumbs up.

* * *

The sun rose above the horizon to the sound of the helicopter lifting into the air, swooping, turning, coming in low then raising the nose, which was a defensive maneuver if the copter was being shot at from ground level. Fifteen minutes passed until the copter landed. The Ukrainian pilot shook hands with Prescott and left the MI-8.

"He's good," the pilot said to Logan. "Load up and have a good flight." He gripped Petro's hand. "Come back with us, I have a bad feeling in my bones about this."

"I'm committed, Valkie. I've told everyone you are in charge while I'm gone. We'll keep in touch with the phones, my friend, and don't worry, I plan on coming back in one, live piece."

* * *

Aafreen quickly walked to the elder's hut. She patted the straw next to the doorway and was told to enter. The elder sat in a dark corner drinking tea and when he saw who it was, poured another cup and handed it to her. "You have news?"

"My brother just called me. We should see them in an hour or two. He's coming by helicopter and the rest of his men are coming in trucks and bringing the weapons."

"Does he know the makeup of our fighters?" The elder asked, insinuating out of thirty-seven fighters, thirteen were women and only one man out of the entire group had been in modern fighting with weapons.

"Ah, no. It will make no difference as he would have come if there were only the men or only women." Her face brightened. "The women fighters will be a bonus!"

"Yes, I'm sure. Tell everyone about them coming. No tribal dances or celebrations, as this is no time to celebrate. After the battle, we'll dance," the elder said. He raised his cup to Aafreen and they both sipped the tea. After she left his hut, the elder said in a low voice, "God be with us."

Chapter Thirteen

The helicopter skirted the village before landing. Dust blew up blinding the natives who had come to watch them land. After the engines shut down, Jean Paul was the first to leave the helicopter. Aafreen ran from the group and threw her arms around him.

"Jean Paul, Jean Paul, my brother!" She squeezed him as he hugged her back.

"Aafreen, my sister," he said. Tears ran down his cheeks. "Where's mother and Cabriol?"

Suddenly, he was hugged and kissed by his mother and younger sister. He looked to Logan, who motioned him to leave with the three. Jean Paul, with his arms around his mother, Aafreen and Cabriol, moved away from the helicopter and the eyes of the natives watching them.

Omallia came forward with his hand out. "We're glad to see you. It has been very tense in our waiting. What can we do?"

Logan shook his hand and said, "Let's get these supplies unloaded. The convoy should be here in a couple of hours. First thing we do after they get here is take you out and show you how to shoot the rifles."

Omallia nodded. "Good. You were told we have twenty-four men ready to fight." After a pause, and seeing Logan's questioning gaze, he added, "and thirteen women."

"Not to seem discourteous, but did you say thirteen women?" Logan asked, disbelief on his face.

"Yes, twenty-four men and thirteen women."

"Holy shit. Sorry, I didn't mean it to sound that way. We were expecting more men," Logan said.

"Some didn't have the courage, or were too old. The women are strong... and brave. Don't worry, the women, like the men, will fight to the death," Omallia said with conviction.

"Okay, enough said." Logan oversaw the unloading of one hundred MRE's, or, Meals Ready to Eat, and several crates of rifles and ammunition from the helicopter. "We've brought enough food for you to join us and have food for several months. The majority will be on the trucks coming."

Petro approached Logan and pulled him to the side. "Jean Paul gave me his iPad to give you. Here's the code. He wants you to check the satellite position of the Janjaweed."

Logan took the iPad and poked the code in. A satellite view came into the screen showing several islands and some ships docked at a port. "What the hell?" He exited, then put the code in again. The same picture came up. "Where's Jean Paul?" Petro pointed to a hut.

"Jean Paul," Logan said at the doorway. He was invited in by Aafreen and asked if he'd like some tea. He shook his head and said, "We have a problem, the satellite's moved."

"What?"

"The satellite's moved. It's showing some islands and boats. Here," Logan said, handing him the iPad. "You try it, maybe I didn't get it right."

The same view came up for Jean Paul. "Damn. Hold on for a minute." He took the satellite phone from his belt holder and pushed some numbers. "Terry, sorry to bother you so late. We haven't the satellite images anymore, what's going on?" He listened for a minute then said, "All right, I'll be waiting."

Logan stepped out of the hut and called Petro over. "We have some problems, no up to date info on the location of the Janjaweed. How about taking the copter and do some recon? Stay as far away as you can. We just need to know about how far out they are from the village."

He handed the Ukrainian a map and told him Prescott was tying the copter down, so he should kick it in gear. He went back into the hut and saw Jean Paul on the phone. "Yes, I understand, Terry, there's only so much you can do. Do you know who ordered the change? I see. Well, if you can, try to keep any attention away from us. Time is growing short before we engage."

The sound of the helicopter rumbled through the hut walls. Jean Paul looked up in surprise. "We're having them go out and try to find where the Janjaweed are. We need to have some sort of idea how close they are," Logan said. "Apparently no more satellite pictures?"

"The CIA requested surveillance over some Japanese Islands that are close to North Korea. Nothing he can do about it," Jean Paul said.

"A little suspicious timing, I'd say. I wonder if the FBI could be involved? Shelby said they'd had his room bugged and tried following him."

Jean Paul looked out the door and watched the helicopter disappear to the north. "There's nothing they can do to us here, for the time being. Perhaps when we get back, but we'll cross that road when we come to it. I'll have Reynolds get our law firm working on some possibilities. I promise everyone will be legally protected."

"We aren't worried about that. There's a job to do. When the rest of the guys get here, we'll start getting the natives familiar with the rifles and pistols. I'll set perimeter guards with radios out far enough to give us an early warning if we're going to be attacked."

* * *

Prescott flew the helicopter low until they came to a high ridge about thirty miles from the village. He set it down behind a small bluff. "Let's take us a look-see," he said. Killing the engine they climbed out and trotted to the base of the bluff, then began climbing up the gentle rise. Petro reached the top and put his hand down to help Prescott up the last few feet. They hunkered over as they ran to the edge overlooking a small valley.

"Oh... my... God!" Petro whispered.

Chapter Fourteen

Below them, in the shallow valley, small fires in front of tents glowed like a swarm of lightning bugs. "There must be a hundred tents down there," Petro said. He pointed his finger. "I don't know how many horses and camels are down there, but enough to make it scary."

"Too bad we don't have some bombs," Prescott said, "cuz we could blow most of them to hell right now. That'd change the odds." He stood up and shielded his eyes with a hand. "Look."

About a dozen men with rifles in their hands were climbing on horses. They took off in a gallop towards the ridge Petro and Prescott stood on.

"I think they're coming after us, or at least to check out the noise the copter made landing. We better get out of here," Prescott said, heading toward the helicopter.

After they climbed in and Prescott fired the engine, he turned to Petro. "We've got a couple of AK-47's in the ship. Why don't I swoop down on them and you see if your aim is any good?"

"Damn, Lee, I like your attitude. Give me a second to get the rifles and buckled in."

Prescott lifted the MI-8 off the ground in a low circle, pointed the nose to the opposite end of the ridge from where they had stood, then, as they flew past the end of the ridge, dropped towards the valley. He cut power and let the helicopter basically auto-rotate down, pointing at the horseback riders coming in their direction. The sound of gunfire could be heard in the cabin.

"The sons-of-bitches are firing at us," Prescott yelled to Petro. "Give 'em something to think about, Petro."

Prescott shoved the throttle full open and leveled out. Petro, with an AK-47 on full automatic and a seventy-five round drum loaded, squeezed the trigger. Dirt blew up by the horses until he made a slight adjustment. Men's arms flew into the air as they were shot off their horses. Some of the horses stumbled and went down, throwing their riders. Another burst of automatic fire from Petro hit four more riders. He reloaded another drum and fired at the remaining three riders who had turned and were racing back towards the camp, the riders leaning low over the horses' necks.

"Yeehah! That's some damn fine shooting, partner," Prescott shouted while pumping his fist. The MI-8 shook as it made a hard half circle, climbing up and over the ridge. "Don't want them to see what direction we're going."

Fifteen minutes later, the helicopter landed on the outskirts of the village. Logan, with Shelby, who had just arrived, met them at the landing area.

"What'd you see?" Logan asked. He saw a couple of bullet holes in the fuselage of the copter.

"There are hundreds of them," Petro said. "I'd have to say two, three, maybe even four hundred or more. They're camped out below a ridge about thirty or forty miles from here. Let me tell you, Logan, it's spooky how many of them there are."

Prescott spoke up, "Don't forget there's about ten less of them heathens, Petro."

"What do you mean?" Logan asked.

"We had some of them come after us," Prescott said, " and with Petro's good shooting, he took around ten or so out of the picture. The guy's a damn fine shooter, let me tell you."

"I wasn't planning on having a shoot-out yet," Logan said, "But, what the hell, might as well show 'em what they're going to come up against. Any suggestions since you guys had the first contact?"

"Yeah," Prescott said. "Put a couple of machine guns in the copter and we'll blow the holy shit out them. Trust me, that's what we did in Vietnam, when the politicians didn't stick their butts in."

Logan told them to hold on for minute and went over to a young man dressed in fatigues and a bandanna over his head. After talking and gesturing, the man nodded and walked towards the trucks where the weapons were being unloaded. Logan walked back to Prescott, Shelby and Petro. "Riley over there is going to sling a M-30 on each side of the cargo doors. Will that work for you?" Logan asked.

"Yeah, it will," Prescott answered. "Too bad you don't have any .50 calibers, but beggars can't be choosers. Once the .30's are in, we can fly back and cut the numbers down some." The old pilot was almost panting. "Damn, I hope all this excitement don't give me a heart attack."

Everyone turned and stared at him. "Just fooling you. I'm in great shape for a sixty-five year old," Prescott said, lighting a cigarette.

"Sixty-five? You old bastard," Shelby said. "You told me you were fifty-six and didn't smoke."

"A little old to believe in fairy tales, ain't ya, kid?"

There was a moment of silence then an outbreak of hard laughter. Shelby wiped tears from his eyes and walked across the village to where Samantha was talking with Molly Southfield, the ex-army physician's assistant and helping put medical supplies in a hut. He grabbed some boxes and stacked them next to others inside.

"Go for a walk with me," he said. The sun was easing down behind the far mountains and he knew the helicopter wouldn't be flying at night.

Sam told Molly she'd be back in a little while and walked with Shelby out into the desert. "It's beautiful here, in its own way," she said, taking his hand.

"I've noticed Petro has been quite attentive. Am I in a competition?" Shelby asked. He pulled her in to him and kissed her hard.

She responded by biting his lip and pushed him back when he yelped. "What the hell, Sam."

"Shelby, I love you, but I also have feelings for Petro. When you were in prison, I worked with him when Daddy had a deal going. We're close, but in all honesty, there's just something about ex-cons with one leg that turns me on." She laughed and trotted back to the village.

He caught her near the hut. "You need to tell Petro. I like the guy, and I know damn good and well he has some pretty deep feelings for you."

"Okay, I will, tomorrow."

"No, tonight."

"Don't think you can make or put demands on me, Shelby. I said tomorrow and that's when I'll talk to him. Now, shut the hell up." She went into the hut.

He walked in the direction of the helicopter trying to decide if he needed to worry more about Samantha and Petro or if the feds were still trying find him. Probably better worry about the two of them, he thought. The feds wouldn't be wasting any more time on me.

Chapter Fifteen

Special Agent in Charge Edward Cosworth picked the phone up. "Director Beningham, please give me some good news."

Central Intelligence Agency Assistant Director, Arthur Beningham, in charge of satellite surveillance, said, "I don't know if it's good news, Agent Cosworth, but due to a change in the actions of North Korea, we moved our satellite from Darfur to an area over North Korea."

"Great! I've no doubt you'll investigate why that satellite was ordered to monitor a piece of desert over Africa," Cosworth said. His voice almost cackled from joy while he rubbed his chest.

"Umm, no. We were requested by the Senate Intelligence Committee to position the satellite over a particular area of Darfur, to track a possible attack on natives by a government backed Islamic group. There was nothing illegal or inappropriate in the request." Beningham took a long breath then said. "I can't divulge any other information to you, Agent Cosworth, national security, you know."

The blood drained out of Cosworth's face. He was getting damn tired of being told the FBI wasn't privy to confidential information. Who the hell did they think they were? "Don't forget who you're dealing with. This is the Federal Bureau of Investigation, and I—"

"And don't forget who you are talking to, Agent Cosworth. The Central Intelligence Agency. Good day." Beningham hung the phone up.

Cosworth slammed his phone down. At that moment, Spurlock knocked on his door. "Come in and have something, please," Cosworth said.

"We have a face recognition match on Donavan, chief. Donovan purchased a ticket at LaGuardia using the alias of Tony Burma on Air Canada to Toronto." He placed a photograph on Cosworth's desk. "We think he was with this woman, Samantha Pershing." Another photo was placed next to Donavan's.

Cosworth picked the photos up and looked hard at them. "Who did you say was the woman?"

"Her name is Samantha Pershing, a psychologist who works with injured veterans. He met her at Walter Reed and she visited him in prison."

"Good work. Have you found where they went?"

"Good news and bad news," Spurlock said. "They chartered a jet and the flight plan was to Africa."

"Africa? What the hell is he doing going to Africa?" Cosworth said. "Sorry for interrupting, go on."

"The jet fueled at Dakar, Donavan and Pershing went through customs, then they flew in the jet to Birao, Central African Republic. Now the bad news," Spurlock said, putting a file on the desk. "The jet was shot down at the airport. The authorities said rebels were attacking the airport and fired some kind of missile that hit the jet while it was in the air. There were no survivors."

"Can we get DNA from the bodies for a positive identification?"

Spurlock shook his head. "The jet was blown to bits, then the pieces hit the ground and burned. No one put it out because of the fighting. Jet fuel burns at a high temperature, you know. There was nothing left of the victims but ash."

"What can I say? There is a God." Cosworth smiled. "I think we can close the case file on Shelby Donavan, now. Good work, Arnie." He took a bottle of Tums of the front desk drawer and threw four into his mouth.

"You okay, chief? You're looking a little pale." Spurlock thought it was from being such a cold-hearted bastard after his statement about Donavan being dead.

"I'm fine, just some indigestion problems, probably from the excitement. I'm going to get a doctor's appointment to get checked out," Cosworth replied.

After Spurlock left his office, Cosworth put the all of Donavan's files in his briefcase. With the odd events of other U.S. agencies not being cooperative with him, he would put the files in a safe place at home until, in his mind, there could not be any doubt to the exit from this world of Shelby Donavan.

On the drive to his home, he thought about Jean Paul Allahamba's business jet at the Pennsylvania airport where Donavan was taken. One rule is don't believe in coincidences, he thought. The jet flew Donavan to Newark. But, why? A billionaire who owns a broadcasting company keeping company with a convicted gun smuggler doesn't make sense. Allahamba had enough money to buy any weapon he wanted without a middle man. He could buy an arms company if he wanted, so, once again, why Donavan?

He pulled into the garage, shut the car off, grabbed the briefcase and trudged into his house. Ever since his wife of thirty-five years had died from cancer, Cosworth's life was his work. To be a Special Agent in Charge brought perks and attention. Once, he'd been asked by the POTUS about a case he was working involving bribes being offered to Congressmen. The highlight of his career.

Inside the house, he put his briefcase down on the kitchen counter, walked to the den, opened up the liquor cabinet, and poured himself a large glass of bourbon. He sat down in his leather recliner then got up, retrieved his briefcase, sat back down in the recliner and took a folder out of the briefcase. Prison records, interviews, court documents, all having to do with Shelby Donavan filled the folder. Donovan had been offered a reduced sentence if he would become a confidential informant – getting and giving evidence on the person or persons supplying him the weapons he sold. Cosworth didn't care that the weapons were sold to fighters trying to defend themselves from murdering radicals who killed anyone they saw except for young girls. The girls were taken, raped and then sold into slavery. That wasn't his jurisdiction… too bad it was happening but that didn't allow Donavan to break the law.

Cosworth took another sip of his drink and grimaced. Sweat broke out and beaded on his face. A dull pain radiated in his jaw and down his left arm. Great, he thought. I'm getting a heart attack. The telephone sat on an end table across the room next to the couch. Cosworth collapsed just as he reached for the phone, knocking the handset off the base. He crawled to the phone and poked 911.

Please, God. Not now, I'm not finished, he thought as the pain intensified. He lost consciousness the same time as the emergency operator answered the call.

* * *

Special Agent Spurlock sat in the waiting room of the Mount Sinai Beth Israel hospital talking into his cell phone. "Yeah, the doctors think he had a massive coronary. Uh huh, he's still in ICU. No, they won't tell me anything." Spurlock ended the call and as he was waiting for the elevator, a doctor approached and told him Cosworth was in a coma and unresponsive. He wouldn't give a prognosis on the odds of his recovery. Spurlock thanked him and left the hospital. Different emotions ran through him. Even though Cosworth could piss him off to the ninth degree, the man believed in the law. Now, I don't necessarily go by every rule, Spurlock thought. Sometimes you have to bend the rules.

His cell phone rang and when he answered the night shift agent told him files were missing and ordered him to go to the SAC's home and see if he could locate them.

At Cosworth's house, the special agent searched every room, opened all the cupboards, checked all the bookcases after taking the hundreds of books out, and came up with a big fat nothing. The briefcase was empty. Spurlock was told the missing files had to do with a current investigation Cosworth had just started. Of course. Donavan. When the man was released from prison without explanation, the agent-in-charge almost choked on his anger.

His cell phone rang. "Spurlock," he answered. "Yes, okay, okay. Nothing here, I'm going to go back to the office and look some more." Tears eased down his cheeks. "You just had to go and die, didn't you, chief?"

An hour and forty-five minutes later he was sitting at his desk; hand on the back of his neck holding a wet, cold towel. Something nagged at the back of his mind, but he couldn't quite bring it to his consciousness. Something Cosworth had given him about six months ago. Something he'd said, "a little place that comes in handy every once in a while." What the hell was he talking about?

A few minutes after midnight Spurlock decided to go home. Maybe a drink and some sleep would help him remember.

After his wife had divorced him, he downsized to a small one bedroom apartment in the west side suburbs. His kitchen table served as his home office. He sipped a glass of bourbon and walked to a corner of the room where a five drawer file cabinet stood. Bending over, he opened the bottom drawer that had dozens of stacked file folders. A notebook sat on the top. Spurlock picked up the notebook and thumbed through the pages. "Got it!" He pulled his coat on, jogged downstairs and outside to the parking lot, where he climbed into his car and headed down 15th Avenue.

Forty minutes later he entered Cosworth's house and turned on the lights in the den. He went straight to the bookshelf, swept a row of books off and pulled the backing off, revealing the safe door. With the notebook in his hand, he dialed the numbers into the combination dial, heard a heavy click then pulled the door open.

Empty! What the hell, the damn safe was empty. Spurlock slammed the door shut. I give up, he thought, turning to leave. Screw it; I'll have a drink for him. He took a glass and put two inches of bourbon in from the bottle on the liquor cabinet and then flopped down in the leather recliner. "Here's to you, chief," he said, taking an inch of the bourbon in a long sip. His hand felt the lever and he pulled it back, reclining the chair. Glancing over the arm, he saw a folder on the floor. "Are you kidding me?" Picking the folder up he saw it was the case file on Donavan. "I'm going to work this case for you chief. I won't let you down."

With a tight grip on the folder, Spurlock turned off the lights and left the house.

* * *

He couldn't believe finding the files on the floor, all of them on Donavan. Grabbing Cosworth's briefcase, he shoved the files inside and decided in honor of Cosworth, he was going to find out what the hell was going on with World Wide Communications and Donavan. Why, he thought, would there be an association of the two? No matter, he'd find out first about the Pershing woman, then track down where they flew to. The FBI had sources, like Interpol. Yeah, look out, I'm coming after you.

The time was a little after midnight when Spurlock left Cosworth's house and headed back to his apartment. Wentworth Street came up and he turned onto the road, deciding he'd take a short cut, even though it crossed through a tough part of the city called Division. More than half the street lights were either burnt out or busted out, making the streets dark with heavy shadows. Groups of young men huddled in front of bars and low rider cars smoked rubber as they left stop lights.

His police scanner blared out a stolen aviation fuel tank truck alert. Last seen heading east on 121st Street, about five blocks from where he was driving. Turning the red lights in the grill on, he hung a fast left and went west on Burmese Avenue, towards the last location of the truck. His heart rate picked up from the building excitement, and he loved it.

When Spurlock raced across 120th Street, the tanker, going 45mph, hit the driver's door of his car, rolling it over and shoving it down the street and into a light post. The tanker's back end swung around hitting the post and splitting the fuel compartment open. 105 octane jet fuel spewed out over Spurlock's car and when the fumes hit the engine, flashed into a spreading, hot fire. The driver and passenger in the truck jumped out and ran down the street, ignoring Spurlock's screams as the fire consumed his car. His safety belt had jammed and wouldn't release.

* * *

After the car fire was extinguished by the fire department, ten minutes later, the coroner peered into the car. Spurlock's charred body sat on the burned seat springs. Everything inside the car was ash.

"The poor bastard," the coroner said. "We have to let the body cool off before we can move it." Pointing a finger at the police on the scene, he said, "I guess you'll have to try and trace the car to hopefully be able to identify him. At least I think it's a him."

Chapter Sixteen

A day later, when dawn broke in the village, the sound of the helicopter's twin turbine engine turning over woke up anyone still asleep. Petro was dressed in combat gear and climbed into the cargo seats near a side door and checked the .30 caliber machine gun. He stuck a thumb up. "Everything's good to go."

"Just a sec, we got company coming," Prescott said.

The young soldier, Donald Riley, who had put the machine guns on slings in the copter, trotted up to the copter and climbed in the side opposite Petro. "I'm going with you, I already cleared it with Logan." He strapped in and put the intercom earphones on. With a thumb up, he said, "Let's go get them suckers."

Prescott lifted off, made a slow circle and headed towards the Janjaweed camp. He leveled off at fifty feet and told the other two he was going to stay low then come up the ridge from the camp's blind side.

"Why are you here, Riley?" Petro asked. "You've already seen combat. You haven't had your fill yet?"

"I'll tell you after you tell me why I don't hear hardly any accent. Logan said you're a Ukrainian."

"When someone spends seven years in the states going to college, working in restaurants and talking nothing but English, a person begins speaking it pretty good."

"Makes sense," Riley said. He slid his hand up and down the breech of the machine gun.

"So, like I asked, why are you here?"

"I love action, hell, I need it, man. For two years I was higher than shit on dope and fighting the Afghanis. Pretty much got off the dope, but still love the fighting. Tried getting on with the cops in Chicago, but I flunked the psych test. Some doctors thought I was too aggressive and might be trigger happy. Figured they could kiss my ass. Kept in touch with some guys and shazam, here I am." He took a can of Skoal out of his pocket, popped the top, took a pinch out and shoved it deep into his lower lip.

"You're off the dope, you said, right?"

The MI-8 reached the base of the ridge and climbed nearly straight up until they reached the top.

"Like I said, pretty much." He straightened up and pointed. "Bogies at three o'clock." Riley yelled, slamming the bolt back on the .30 caliber and pulled the trigger.

Petro did the same, and moved the machine gun back and forth while the shells flew in the cabin. "They were waiting for us, goddamn it."

Bullets struck the helicopter from automatic fire. Riley yelled he was hit and blood sprayed the cabin wall. He kept firing with one hand, swiveling the gun on the sling.

"Lee, get us the hell out of here," Petro shouted. The copter banked hard and the engine howled as Prescott shoved the throttle full open on the big, bulky, helicopter. Bullets blew through the fuselage of the helicopter. Petro yipped as a round took the end off of his little finger. He grabbed the stub and squeezed the blood flow off. The helicopter dead dropped over the side of the ridge until almost crashing into the rocks below when Prescott pulled the stick back. He leveled the copter out and with full throttle, guided the old MI-8 back to the village.

"Get some altitude!" Petro shouted.

"No, it'll be too easy to hit us with a RPG. Shut the hell up, I'm flying this bird," Prescott said. He had the copter making a long "s" maneuver as he aimed in the direction of the village. Two explosions hit the ground where the copter had been a moment before. "There's the RPGs." He suddenly pulled the stick back and the copter lifted, then dropped the nose as he swung left and right.

Prescott blew his breath out. "I think we made it. How's the kid?"

Petro had unbuckled and sat next to Riley holding pressure over the wound in his right shoulder area with a bandage. Riley's eyes were closed and his face had a chalky white cast on it. "He's been hit hard, Lee. We have to get him back fast." Petro tied a bandage around his finger, gritting his teeth from the pain.

"Have the old gal going full throttle. Keep him alive for ten more minutes. I'm radioing the village to have the girl standing by." He picked the handheld up and spoke into it. Putting it down, he said, "I got a hold of them. Molly's ready. Keep him alive, Petro."

* * *

There was a small group standing by the landing area when the helicopter came in for the landing. When it touched down, Molly, and two men carrying a stretcher, ran to the side where a cargo door slid open and Petro waved his hand. They carried Riley out of the helicopter and laid him on the stretcher while Molly kept the pressure on the gunshot wound. "No bubbles coming out of his mouth, so I don't think his lung was hit," she said. Riley was taken to the first aid tent where she checked him for any other wounds. "He'll live," she said.

Logan gathered the men around him. "Tomorrow, we'll show the natives how to fire the guns and reload. This is make or break for us. The copter will go up again to see if they can ambush the bunch of them. A squad will go out and engage the Janjaweed as far from the village as we can make it. Remember, our mission is to take them out so they won't want to invade the village. Any questions?"

A soldier raised his hand. "Any restrictions when we engage them?"

There was silence in the group. Some looked away and others gave their attention to Logan, waiting for a response.

"No. We want to kill or maim as many as we can. Remember, they invade villages, burn them down, rape the women and the children, and do it in the supposedly name of God or some bullshit reason. Screw that. Anyone disagree?" Logan asked.

"No," a roar of voices shot back.

"As you know, Riley was wounded this morning. He's going to be okay, and says we need to take these bastards out. I agree, how about you?"

Fists flew into the air as another roar of voices shouted, "Kill them all," "Remember Riley," "Protect the village." One man, whose name was Alfred Banjune, a slight black man, stepped forward and said, "This is what fighting for democracy is. Not to let the powerful set the rules, but for everyone to have an even shot at life without fear of interference from a government. At least that's my take on it."

Heads nodded in agreement. The meeting broke up with a robust feeling of doing good against evil, as phony as it sounded. There were no parameters of what could be done to protect the village and their people.

* * *

Petro went into Logan's hut, a troubled look on his face.

"What's up," Logan asked.

"I think they knew we were coming. Why would they be on top of the ridge when we got there? If Prescott wasn't one hell of a pilot, we'd been down and dead."

"Sounds to me like we have a traitor with us. What do you think?"

"I don't know," Petro answered. "Only a satellite phone could have been used if somebody contacted the Janjaweed force by wireless. Otherwise, there would have been someone going to their camp, I'd think."

"We only have one satellite phone, I'll check the outgoing calls. If we have a traitor, that's going to be a huge, dangerous problem," Logan said. "We need to find him... or her."

"If it's a him, who knows? You get into Christian and Islamic religions, it's a crap shoot on what someone thinks is the god-accepted way of doing things. I don't even like to think about it."

"We have to find out if there is a snitch, who the hell it is," Logan said. "Our lives depend on it."

Chapter Seventeen

After the meeting broke up, Alfred Banjune, the slim, black soldier, felt a hand on his shoulder. He turned and saw Jean Paul's sister, Cabriol, smiling at him.

"You speak from your heart," she said. "And looking into your eyes, you've seen things because your eyes are weary."

"Probably from growing up in a big city, black slum, and being in the army for twenty years." He gently took her hand and began walking through the village. "I've been watching you since we arrived. No offense, but you can't fire a rifle with those hands, so why are you still here in the danger zone?"

"I won't leave my sister and mother. I told Logan I wanted to carry ammunition when the fighting starts, but he doesn't think I can do it. There must be some way I can, wouldn't you think?"

"Possibly, let me think about it as we walk." He paused walking. "For some reason, I feel comfortable with you," Banjune said. "I was born in South Darfur."

"Really, a village or city?" Cabriol asked. Once or twice their hips touched and she quickly moved aside, looking about her to see if anyone had seen.

"A village called Tal Bileil, east of the Marra Mountains. My parents were killed and my grandparents fled with me to Boro City. There wasn't enough food or water so they took me to Chad where we were able to be smuggled into the United States. They actually met your brother in New York in 1988.

He'd started an organization called Africans from Darfur, that assisted Africans to assimilate into the United States and eventually get citizenship. It was through my grandparents that I met Jean Paul and one of the reasons I'm here is to pay him back for his generosity in helping my Papa and Gram... and get back at the Janjaweed for what they've done to so many natives."

"Strange, isn't it? You're here to repay a debt and get revenge. And now we meet under these circumstances. What a small world." They continued to walk around the village, talking quietly and feeling more and more at ease with each other.

"I have an idea for you," Banjune said. "We get, now don't become offended, something similar to an oxen yoke, but smaller, and of course, lighter. That way you can put it on your shoulders and hang the ammo boxes from the beams. You should be able to carry two boxes. What do you think?" A huge smile crossed his face, and it seemed there was a twinkle in his eyes.

"If Logan lets me, I think it's a wonderful idea. I'm beginning to think we met for a reason," she said. "Let's go talk to him now." They turned around and headed back to the huts the soldiers used.

* * *

"So, we have to find out if someone contacted the Janjaweed and told them about the flight today. I have a hard time believing they would be on top of the ridge on the chance we'd be back in the same place," Logan said to a small group of men. "Shelby, what do you think?"

"Sorry, but we can't know if they'd come back to the ridge on their own or if they'd been warned. Who here knows what the hell those Arabs think?" No one said anything. He continued, "I don't know. Let's try an old and true disinformation plan. We'll have a meeting, tell where we'll be going with the helicopter, and find out if the Arabs show up. If they do, we have a traitor, if not, all we did is waste a little time."

"What if we say we're going to the ridge again, then have the helicopter come in high enough to see if they're there and still be far enough away to be safe from gunfire," Jack Hagel said, a man who had served with Logan in Iraq.

"The problem with that, Jack," Shelby said, "is how do we know they aren't still on top of the ridge? How about we say we're going to move some men to the base of the ridge on foot? Then use the copter to check it out."

"I like that," Hagel said.

"Me, too," Logan put in. "And here's how we catch the traitor, if there is one."

* * *

Three hours later a meeting was called in the center of the village. Logan announced they were going to send a small group of men to the base of the ridge to set up an ambush. They would use one of the trucks to get within a couple of miles, then hike the rest of the way. The team would be leaving before daybreak.

Later, with a moonless, dark night, eight nearly invisible men hid in brush and desert grass four hundred yards from the village. They were situated so they could use the night vision goggles to see if anyone left the village. As hours passed, nothing except a small herd of white-eared kob were seen by the men. When the truck left with eight men in it, they waited to see if anyone followed. No one did.

After the truck was out of sight of the village, it drove ten more miles and then parked behind a small copse of acacia trees. The driver turned the engine off and took the cup of coffee from the soldier in the passenger seat. "Might as well get comfortable for a couple of hours," the driver said, taking a sip of coffee. The six men in the back got out and formed a perimeter guard.

As the sun came up, the helicopter, fueled from the fuel tank truck, lifted off with Shelby and Petro manning the two .30 caliber machine guns. Both of them had binoculars strapped around their necks and Prescott gained altitude in a sweeping turn.

Cruising at six thousand feet altitude, with the sun at their backs, the helicopter came onto the ridge below them. Petro and Shelby had the binoculars to their eyes.

"Look!" Shelby shouted the same time flashes could be seen from the bottom of the ridge. The .30 calibers started firing, raking the area the fighters were shooting from. Both Petro and Shelby emptied the ammo cans with the belts of bullets, then yelling at Prescott to get them the hell out of there. A quick turn and the helicopter headed back towards the village. Dust floated in the air below them from close to fifty horses and camels, being ridden by the Janjaweed carrying rifles. Between the riders and the village, the truck could be seen in the distance.

"No way they could have been in the camp when we flew over the ridge. They knew, dammit." Shelby picked the radio up. "Copter to Logan, copter to Logan."

Static, then, "Go ahead, Shelby."

"Notify the truck there's at least fifty Janjaweed a mile away and coming their way, fast. They need to get back to the camp, now. We're out of ammo. Copy?"

"Copy. The truck won't start. I'll have them dig in and we're on our way. Do anything you can to help them. Out," Logan said. The radio went dead.

"What can we do, Lee?" Shelby yelled. He took his Glock out of the holster and put the extra mags on his lap. Petro saw him and did the same.

"I'm gonna come in behind them. See if you can pick some off. We'll be going full throttle, I don't want to eat a rocket." Prescott banked the copter and made a long loop as he gained altitude. As he passed the horseback riders, he banked again, slammed the throttle open and dived towards the back of the pack. He leveled out, shouted at Shelby and Petro to fire and held the bird level.

The sharp crack of gunfire filled the cabin. Spent shells from the pistols bounced off the metal sides of the helicopter as Petro and Shelby fired the Glocks as fast as they could pull the triggers. Each emptied the pistols, reload two other times and fired at the riders below them. Some tried returning the fire, some were shot off their horses, but nearly all bore down on the truck when Shelby and Petro ran out of bullets. Prescott buzzed the tail end of the riders, spooking their horses into scattering away to the sides of the main force.

"We're getting hit, I'm getting us out of here," Prescott yelled. He banked and pulled the nose up. A half dozen holes appeared in the rear cabin. "You guys okay?"

"Yeah," Petro replied. "We have to do something, the war's starting. Look!" They saw the Janjaweed ride into the area of the truck at a full gallop, every man shooting rifles while they rode.

The men on the ground returned fire bringing down horses and Arabs. One soldier on the ground stood up as the Arabs raced past, firing his AK-47 into the riders. Two fell from their horses to the ground. One rider pulled his horse into a quick circle firing as he turned. The soldier, still standing and firing, dropped his rifle and collapsed to the ground.

"Hang on!" Prescott yelled again. He brought the helicopter down close to the ground between the soldiers and the Janjaweed, the blades blowing sand and dust into the horseback riders. Some of Arabs fired blindly in the direction of the helicopter while most of the horses fought to get away from the blowing sand. They began galloping and scattering in all directions from the truck and helicopter. Prescott kept the helicopter circling low to the ground. "If the guys can see what I'm doing, grab 'em and drag them into the bird."

Petro and Shelby both opened their doors and yelled at the soldiers while the helicopter crabbed sideways towards the truck. "They don't know what we're doing, too much sand to see us waving," Shelby said. He jumped out and hit the ground running.

"Shelby, Goddammit, Shelby!" Petro screamed at him. He heard some gunshots and Shelby disappeared into the cloud of sand.

Chapter Eighteen

The horn blasted which signaled everyone to assemble at the vehicles. Alfred Banjune told Cabriol he had to go, and took off running.

She waved as he left, and said, "God be with you, Alfred, and be safe."

At the assembly area, men were loading weapons and scrambling inside the trucks, dressed in battle gear and flak jackets. Banjune grabbed his weapon, gear and jumped in the closest truck to him.

Logan had a bullhorn and said to the natives, "Get your weapons, keep behind the cover of the sandbags, and stay alert. The village might be attacked." He held up the radio. "Aafreen has a radio and will stay in contact with us. We have to go, now!" The door slammed as he climbed into the UAZ with a .30 caliber machine gun mounted on the half cab roof. The other six GAZ light armored trucks and remaining UAZ threw dirt into the air as they took off and headed towards their stranded comrades fighting for their lives.

* * *

Prescott keep the helicopter circling, throwing up a sand cloud obscuring both the soldiers and them. Petro couldn't see Shelby after he'd disappeared into the cloud, but the sound of gunshots were heard and bullets hitting the fuselage of the helicopter were felt. The radio gave out a squeal of static, rising and falling, then

Logan's voice. "We're just about there, what's the situation?"

Petro responded, telling them they were waiting for Shelby who was trying to guide the soldiers to the helicopter, and to hurry their asses up, they were being fired on.

Behind the copter, an explosion sent shock waves that rocked the helicopter. "Either our guys fired a RPG or the damn Arabs did." Another explosion, this time farther to the east. "Those are ours," Petro yelled with a laugh. "Get 'em," he said into the radio. "Pull her up, Lee, so we can see what's happening."

The helicopter raised high enough to see the country around them. The Janjaweed were riding in a broken pattern firing their rifles and making the ability to shoot them difficult, though several were seen falling off their horses. Logan and the soldiers were stopped on the perimeter , the machine guns and AK-47's looking like the trucks were a curtain of fire.

"There's Shelby," Petro said, pointing. Shelby had the arm of one soldier over his neck and the other seven putting up cover fire as they ran towards the helicopter. "Set it down, we'll pick them up."

The helicopter dropped down the same time Petro threw the cargo doors open. "Come on," he yelled, jumping out and running towards the men. He heard a burst of gunfire and saw Shelby go down hard, along with the man he was helping. "Shelby!" Petro shouted. The other seven men returned fire, huddling around the two men on the ground.

* * *

Logan's trucks formed a skirmish line and inched forward, firing as they went. Horses shrieked and went down, tossing their riders. When the Arabs stood up, they were hit by a dozen bullets. The remaining riders gathered and galloped to the west. Logan's radio came to life, it was Aafreen.

"Logan, we're being attacked! Help us!" She screamed over the radio. "They're surrounding the village, oh God, hurry!"

He yelled at a man in one of the trucks. "Manny, get six men into the copter, grab two .30's, your AK's and hustle back to the village, they're being attacked. We'll be right behind you." He radioed Prescott and told him the same thing.

Manny nodded, hollered at the soldiers in a truck next to him to bring the guns and get into the helicopter, they had to get back to the village.

Prescott came on the radio and said, "Shelby and another man are down, Logan, Petro went to get them."

"We'll help him, take off and get to the village, fast." Logan saw the last man bail into the helicopter and it lifted off. As soon as the blown sand cleared, Petro was waving at them. He was kneeling down next to two bodies on the ground. "Oh, shit, not you, Shelby." The UAZ and the other trucks sped towards Petro and the two fallen men.

* * *

Prescott had the old bird struggling to fly at 190 knots, with the throttle shoved all the way to max. It shuddered from the strain but she only took eight minutes reach the village. As they approached, natives could be seen hunkered down behind the sand bags filled the day before. A wave of at least one hundred Janjaweed were circling the village, firing rifles as they rode.

Manny yelled at Prescott, "We got the machine guns slung, come in behind them and try to hold the position. We'll blow the holy shit out of them." He slid one cargo door open and another soldier slid the other one open. Manny sat down behind one of the machine guns. Alfred Banjune had the other one. Both of the men pulled the cocking handles back at the same time.

The helicopter swooped in behind the horsemen, Prescott cut the speed the same time the machine guns began firing 650 rounds a minute. Other men, sitting next to the machine guns, cut loose with their AK-47's.

It took a moment for the Janjaweed to notice men were being blown off their horses and some of the horses staggered and fell to the ground. Several riders turned around in their saddles and tried shooting at the helicopter with one hand on their rifles. Out of a hundred riders, at least a third were slaughtered by the automatic weapons from the copter. The remaining Janjaweed turned in a wave and galloped away from the village towards acacia trees that formed a canopy of safety if they could make it.

Prescott banked and lowered the nose. Suddenly, he cut power and turned back to the village.

"What the hell are you doing? We're blowing 'em away. Turn around, Goddammit," Manny yelled at Prescott.

"Can't, the turbo's are overheating. We got to get down, and fast." A high pitched squeal could be heard and the MI-8T dropped fifty feet. The village came into sight just as the copter's engine died. "Hold on, auto-rotation," Prescott yelled at the men, He swung the tail around and the bird landed hard, smoke rolling out of the engine compartment.

Manny had everyone take the weapons from the helicopter and set up a perimeter. He told Alfred and three other men to get the other machine guns and ammo. "I won't be surprised if they try to hit us, so everyone stay alert. If you see them and think you can score a kill, fire away."

* * *

The Janjaweed seemed content to stay three miles from the village, under the acacia trees. If attacked, they would have enough time to escape or counter attack. The leader, Mohammad Huaquin, gathered his men around him.

"They've lost their helicopter, I think. Smoke was coming out of it when they turned away from us. We are powerful, this shows Allah is with us in our mission."

A short, squatty man stepped forward. "We lost a great number of men. We have to bury them. And who knew there would be a military force guarding the village? What are we going to do?"

"First, we come back tonight and bury the brothers we can retrieve, second, we find out how the village will be defended. They're American mercenaries. I don't think they want to die in Darfur trying to protect the African natives. Mount up and we'll ride back to the camp. No more than ten to a group, in case we encounter them."

The horsemen headed for the camp by heading east for two miles before turning north. On the other side of a sunbaked razorback ridge, vehicles could be heard moving towards the village. Huaquin ordered one group to circle behind the trucks and try to shoot as many soldiers as they could, without themselves being killed. The ten men took after the trucks at a hard gallop.

* * *

Logan ran to Petro and kneeled down by Shelby. "How bad?"

"His leg is almost blown off - the other man has been shot in the side, not too bad, I think, but Shelby....

.

"Oh, man, " Shelby moaned. "The son-of-a-bitches shot me in the leg. I'm not sure if I can use it." He rolled over and sat up. "Petro, get me some duct tape and get a truck over here.

"Duct tape? Wait a minute, where's the blood? What the hell's going on with you?" Petro said, his voice raising from confusion as he ran to the closest truck.

Another two soldiers ran over and at Logan's nod, lifted the other man and carried him to the truck that pulled up. Petro climbed out and ran over to Shelby and Logan with a roll of tape, handing it to Shelby.

He began the tape at the top of his thigh, rolled it around in a tight circle, pushed several pieces of his leg back in line and double taped it. When he reached the end of his leg the tape was gone. Logan helped him up and he moved the leg back and forth, though it stuck a couple of times in odd positions.

Petro stared, then said, "You got an artificial leg. I thought you'd bled out and was dead meat, my friend. I never realized."

"Enough talk, let's load up and get back to the village," Logan said. When they got to the trucks, Logan said to the men, "Keep your eyes open, guys, we don't know if they'll try us again on the way back. I haven't heard from Prescott yet. Load up while I call him and get an update if they're not fighting."

He pulled the radio out and talked into it. Nodding his head, he could be heard telling someone they were heading back, no one killed, one injured, so have Molly standing by.

They had driven three or four miles and were passing a ridge when gunfire broke out. The soldiers were being fired on from behind them. Logan stood up, swiveled the machine gun on top of the half cab of the UAZ and cut loose, swiveling the .30 caliber side to side. The other men in the trucks fired also. After two minutes, the gunfire from behind them stopped. A rider-less horse galloped past.

The shooting from the Janjaweed stopped, and they saw the remaining riders heading in the opposite direction.

Logan brushed a hand over his face. "Man, I think we got ourselves into a full blown war."

Chapter Nineteen

The convoy of trucks pulled into the village, dust following close behind them. Molly and Samantha were standing by, a stretcher laying between them. Two men brought the injured soldier from the back of a truck and gently lowered him onto the stretcher. "Lucky he had his flak jacket on," one of the men said as he and the other man picked the stretcher up. With the two women attending, the injured soldier was taken to the hut used for first aid.

Jean Paul, who Logan had stay in the village rather than possibly get in the way if they were in a firefight, walked to the trucks. He carried an AK-47 in one hand and an ammo belt stuffed with magazines in the other. "Logan," he said, a proud look on his face. "We held them off and no one was shot. Thanks to the boys in the helicopter, there's twenty-seven dead Janjaweed and three wounded."

"That's good news, Jean Paul. The first thing we need to do now is take care of the bodies."

"What do you propose we do?"

"Gather 'em up and burn the bodies, down wind," Logan replied. He shouted for the men to come over to him. When they surrounded him, he told them to take two of the cargo trucks and pitch the bodies in the back then take them east about a half mile and stack the bodies in a clearing. Someone would take the fuel tanker with the cargo trucks. "Muslims don't believe in cremation, so we're going to burn the bodies to nothing but ashes."

Jean Paul's face paled, but he nodded his head and followed four men to a cargo truck, pulling on a pair of leather gloves. It took two hours to pick the bodies up and put them in the back of the trucks. Four different times gunshots sounded. "Are they... are they killing some they're finding alive?" Jean Paul asked as he tossed another body into the truck.

"What else you gonna do, use our supplies to fix 'em up, then stick them in jail?" A burley soldier said. His sleeves were rolled up over huge forearms and he tossed bodies like they were made of straw. "Send them back to their buddies? What else you gonna do with them that's safe for us?"

"I hadn't thought of that. There's no recourse except to kill them," Jean Paul said. He continued to walk with the truck and help throw the dead into the back.

Eventually the bodies were stacked like cordwood in a clearing of sand, devoid of the tall desert grass. The fuel tanker fired up its engine, engaged the pump and with a hose, sprayed jet fuel over the dead Janjaweed. Logan came up, struck a fuse and threw it in the middle of the pile. Gray smoke rose and then there was a loud, Whomp! Flames shot up as they spread completely engulfing the bodies. Standing upwind, the men watched as stomachs popped, bodies moved as their ligaments and tendons burned, and skin curled away leaving bones and sinew.

Logan saw Manny and called him over. "We've got to find out who's contacting the Arabs, and how. We've been damn lucky so far, they could have blown the hell out of us if we wouldn't have had the helicopter in the air. They're sneaky, kind of like the Lakota in the old days when they made Custer wonder, where'd all those pissed off Indians come from?"

* * *

Later, after the fire died out, leaving bones and a horrific stink in the air, the men went back to camp and met Logan in an open area away from the village.

"I don't know how it's happening, but someone is telling the Arabs what we're planning," Logan began. "This morning they waited for the helicopter and damn near shot it out of the air over by their camp. Another large band of them slipped around us and attacked the village. All right, let's hear some theories."

Manny spoke up. "No one has seen anyone leaving the village, so whoever it is, has to have some kind of electronic communication. At least, that's what I think."

"You're probably right. Anyone else?" Logan asked.

"No offense Jean Paul, but the guy who's going with your sister didn't fire a shot. I saw him aiming his rifle, but not shooting," a soldier said. He looked embarrassed, but looked Jean Paul in the eye.

"Maybe he just can't kill a person, no matter how evil they are," Jean Paul replied. "I don't know, so I can't make excuses for him."

"How could he contact the Janjaweed?" Logan asked.

After a long pause, Jean Paul said, "Aafreen has a satellite phone. Could he have used it?"

Logan said, "Goddamn, I forgot about that phone. Grab it, Jean Paul, and bring it to me, we'll see if he used it and screwed up by not deleting the calls."

Jean Paul seemed to be deciding, then said, "All right, but until we find evidence, Omallia isn't to be harassed or told of what we're doing. Agreed?"

"Sure, not unless we have proof," Logan said. Looking at the men, he said, "You understand and agree, right? If not, we need to get it resolved."

Everyone nodded or said yes, and the meeting broke up, with the exception of Manny, Logan and Jean Paul.

"If he's dirty, he'll be taken care of, right?" Manny asked.

"This is my call," Logan replied. "If he's dirty, we'll kill the son-of-a-bitch, with no argument. Do you agree, Jean Paul?"

Jean Paul lowered his head as if in prayer, then raised it looked at Manny and said, "If he's guilty, then he's betrayed everyone. He should die." He turned to Logan, and in a soft voice said, "I can't believe I'm saying kill a man, but we don't have another choice."

* * *

Jean Paul asked Aafreen for the satellite phone. She didn't question him but took the phone out of a straw hamper. "Only Omallia and myself know where I keep this," she said, handing her brother the phone.

He turned it on and hit the call log button. A number he didn't recognize was on the list five times. "Did you call this number?" he asked, handing her the phone.

A look of confusion crossed her face. "No, I only have talked to you. I... I don't know this one."

Jean Paul took the phone to Logan and told him what he'd discovered.

Logan took the phone, pushed the call log button, then silently cursed. "I'm gonna call the number." He put the phone number in and hit the 'send' button.

"What news do you have for me?" A deep voice, heavily accented answered.

"The news is I'm going to kill you by putting a bullet in your stinkin' head," Logan said, his teeth gritted.

"Who is this?"

"My name is Logan. I burned your dead and I'm deciding how to screw you from going to heaven and meeting those fat, seventy-two virgins."

There was a pause, then a chuckle. "I am going to enjoy killing you, Logan, of the mysterious group of mercenaries." The phone went dead.

"Manny, go bring Omallia here. Just tell him I want to talk to him," Logan said. Manny nodded and left the area, having another man go with him.

Logan told Jean Paul he should leave, but Jean Paul shook his head.

"I'm part of this. He betrayed all of us and I'd like to hear why."

A half an hour later, Manny came back by himself. "He's not in the camp. I've combed the whole village. I've got some of the other guys looking, too."

Aafreen walked in, eyes red, holding a folded sheet of paper. She handed it to Jean Paul, who opened it, and read. A moment later, he told them, "Omallia has confessed to being a traitor to us. Says he is now Muslim and also follows Islam, like his Janjaweed brothers. He said he assisted his brothers when they ransacked other villages. He suggests we surrender to avoid dying without repenting and not embracing Allah or offending Muhammad." John Paul cleared his throat and muttered, "He also asks Aafreen to join him."

Logan took the letter, quickly read it again, then said, "He's running, probably to the Janjaweed camp." He nodded to Jean Paul and looked at Aafreen. "Why don't you two go have something to eat."

After Jean Paul and his sister left, Logan looked around then said, "Manny, get Alfred, a sniper rifle and see if you can either catch up and take him alive, or kill him. Just be careful in case he's waiting for someone to come after him. We'll take him dead or alive, I don't care which."

* * *

Manny and Alfred took a truck and drove it to a high swell above the desert. They parked, took their weapons and climbed to the top. With binoculars, they scanned the area around them as the sun began dipping down in the west.

"Look!" Alfred said, excitement in his voice. There he is, over there." He pointed to the plains in the east, about twenty miles from the Janjaweed camp.

"I'm surprised they haven't picked him up, thinking we might be after him," Manny said. He took the VEPR Tactical Sniper rifle from the case and wrapped the sling around his arm. "He ain't gonna give up and he's too far away for us to catch up to him. I'm gonna take him out. You got any problem with it?"

"I am going to admit," Alfred said, "me being a Sudanese, Omallia being a Sudanese, I have to say, he ratted us out, kill the son-of -a-bitch. If I could put an RPG up his ass, I would in a heartbeat."

"I'm glad to hear you say that," Manny said. He squinted in the scope, muttering to himself, "A little wind from the right, a tad lower elevation." His finger squeezed the trigger.

Chapter Twenty

Manny squeezed the trigger and the rifle gave a small kick. Looking through the scope, he saw Omallia spin and fall to the ground. "Shit, I nicked him." He jacked another bullet into the chamber and settled into the posture. Relaxed, slow breaths, and loose hands.

Omallia struggled to his feet and looked behind him as he hunkered down near a sparse bush. "Over here, dumb shit," Manny whispered. He squeezed another round off. Omallia jerked then rolled to his side. "I think I got him, but I don't know if I killed him. Com'on, Alfred, let's make sure he's dead," Manny said. He stood up, looked around, walked to the truck and climbed in. Alfred, with his AK-47 at the ready, climbed in the passenger side, sticking his rifle out the window. Manny started the truck, put it in 1st gear and slowly drove towards Omallia.

A few minutes later they pulled up to Omallia, now lying on his stomach. Getting out of the truck, rifles ready, they checked Omallia and saw an exit wound on his back between the shoulders. Alfred checked for a pulse, finding none. "How you got him in the chest while he was lying down is beyond me," Alfred said.

"Because I'm a magnificent shot, my friend," Manny replied. "He was on his forearms, looking at us. I had a big target."

"Yes, you are," Alfred said. "Now what?"

"I'll see what Logan wants to do," Manny said, bringing the radio up to his mouth. "Keep your eyes open, Alfred." He turned to face Omallia's body as he spoke to Logan, nodding his head when Alfred motioned with his hand he was going to climb up a nearby sandy hill.

After reaching the top of the hill, Alfred saw Manny laying some brush over the body, then setting fire to it. The flame licked at the dry brush and flared up, black smoke leading the flames. He turned to look down the hill towards the east and a cold fist squeezed his heart. They were coming, the Janjaweed, and riding fast. They must have been meeting Omallia, that was why he hadn't disappeared into the desert after leaving the village.

Alfred sprinted down the hill, slipped in a small depression in the sand, and tumbled the rest of the way down, hanging on to his rifle the entire time. "Go, they're on the other side of the hill, heading this way," he shouted to Manny. He jumped off the ground and hit a dead run in ten feet, catching Manny, who had taken off the second Alfred had shouted his warning. They reached the truck, hopped in, fired it up and spun the tires turning around the same time bullets hit the truck from gunfire behind them.

* * *

Logan took Jean Paul, Shelby, and Petro to the side and told them Omallia had been killed. "I told them to burn the body," he said, looking at Jean Paul. "We have to make them fear we'll burn everyone we kill and not let them recover the bodies. Try to make their religion work against them."

The voice came over the radio in Logan's hand. "We got a situation here," Manny reported, excitement creeping into his voice. "Coming back to the village as fast as we can, but those damn horses are fast. Give us a hand."

The four leaped into the UAZ, Shelby with a RPG in his hand. Petro yelled to a group of soldiers to standby for a possible attack.

Logan had the UAZ bucking over the newly made two-track. After six miles they could see a cloud of dust coming towards them and hear gunfire in the air. They drove up a slight slope and saw the truck with Manny and Alfred barreling down the trail, two dozen horsemen were behind them and seemed to be closing the distance. Logan slammed on the brakes. "Shelby, put that RPG in the middle of those bastards."

Jean Paul and Petro jumped out of the UAZ with their AK-47's and Logan stood up grabbing the grip of the .30 caliber machine gun mounted on the half roof. "The second our guys are clear, cut loose," Logan ordered. "Wait. What the hell?"

The truck veered left and then right, and went into a slide. The truck's right front and rear wheels lifted into the air as the truck overturned, slamming down into the sand on the driver's side. Alfred stood up through the passenger door window and opened fire with his AK-47.

At the same time Alfred began shooting, Shelby fired the RPG at the band of horsemen, the HE warhead landing in the middle of the riders, exploding and throwing both riders and horses to the ground. Logan pulled the trigger on the machine gun while Petro emptied his rifle's magazine and quickly shoved in another one. He jacked the bolt back and continued firing. Shelby loaded another rocket and fired. Again, an explosion, blowing apart men and animals.

The remaining horsemen turned 180 degrees and galloped back in the direction of their camp. Two more didn't make it as Petro took aim and fired just before they angled behind the sand hill. Jean Paul kept firing at the retreating riders until the magazine was empty.

Logan was out of breath when he reached the overturned truck. Alfred was pulling Manny out of the passenger door. "Give me a hand, he's been shot." Alfred said, holding Manny up with both of his arms around Manny's chest.

Petro and Jean Paul ran up and with Logan, helped Alfred ease Manny out of the truck. They laid him on the ground and Logan checked for a pulse. Blood pumped from his neck. "We got 'em, didn't we," Manny uttered. His eyes closed as he sighed, his body going limp.

"Goddammit, he's dead," Logan said. He cradled Manny's head in his hands and slowly lowered his friend's head down, then gently pulled his hands free. Shelby drove up and got out, looking at the three men surrounding the body.

"I'm sorry, Logan, I truly am," he said, putting a hand on Logan's shoulder.

Logan nodded and stood up. "Take him over by the trees, we'll be right back," he said, grabbing a rifle. "Com'on, Shelby." They climbed in the UAZ, Logan driving, and drove to the area where the Janjaweed bodies had fallen. Getting out, they took a five gallon gas can and walked among them, looking for life.

Alfred, Jean Paul, and Petro heard seven gunshots. A few minutes later, small spirals of smoke rose in the air. "He's burning the dead," Alfred said, "and I'm damn glad." Alfred then looked at Petro. "You're bleeding."

"I cut it on the window when we were pulling him out of the truck." He wrapped his shirt sleeve around the wound.

When Logan and Shelby returned, Manny's body was loaded into the UAZ, then they headed back to the village. Jean Paul's face was ashen.

"I've made a big mistake, " Logan said, driving slow.

"You can't blame yourself," Petro said. "This is war, all of us might die, God forbid."

"I know and my mistake is not taking the fight to them. We should be doing like I said the Indians used to do: sneak attacks, ambushes, hit them when they're not expecting it. I've been too conservative, too much defend rather than being offensive. We're going to change that, now."

They arrived at the village where everyone waited, having heard from Shelby on the radio about Manny being killed. The women of the village said they would prepare him for burial, and took the body to a hut. They would bury him as the sun set, the women said. Aafreen asked the village men to dig a grave, over near an acacia tree, close to the village burial site.

Logan found Prescott at the helicopter, his arms and face covered in oil, a cigarette hanging from his lips. "Had any luck?"

"Yeah, better than you. I'm sorry to hear about Manny, he was a good soldier," Prescott said, turning from Logan for a moment. "That kid, Riley, he worked on copters and was able to find the problem. The quick story is one of the turbo intakes was damaged by bullets and basically with one turbo on and the other out, it went into a dynamic imbalance, is what he said. Anyway, he fixed it. We're ready to see if she'll fly."

* * *

Alfred and Petro carried Manny's body from the UAZ and put him in a burial blanket the women had laid on the ground. With a woman on each corner, they picked him up and took him to the hut for preparation.

Alfred felt a tug on his sleeve. Turning, he put his arms around Cabriol, tears welling in his eyes. She put her arms around him, then stood back and led him away from the soldiers. "I'm so sorry for your friend," she said. "And I'm so grateful to God you're all right." She stretched up and kissed him.

* * *

Samantha and Molly pushed through the crowd to where Shelby and Petro stood talking softly to some soldiers.

"Did either of you get hurt?" Samantha asked. She looked at Shelby with a questioning gaze, then Petro. Both men shook their heads.

"You're bleeding, Petro, let me look at that," Molly said, pulling his shirt sleeve up. An ugly, jagged slice ran down his arm from his elbow to his wrist. His sleeve was soaked with blood. "We have to take care of this, now," she said, guiding him towards the first-aid hut.

Samantha's hand crept into Shelby's. "We were in Iraq together, you know. Logan, Manny and me. Manny was Logan's platoon leader until he was hurt in a firefight. A very loyal soldier, I'll miss him," Shelby said in a whisper. He squeezed Sam's hand. "You also looked at me before Petro."

"So? What about it?"

"He's out, I'm your guy."

* * *

The sun was setting as the villagers and soldiers gathered at the acacia tree by the village graveyard. Every person carried a weapon. As the rays of the sun colored the clouds with fingers of blood red, and high clouds seemed shaped like tears, Manny Rodriquez, wrapped in a traditional burial blanket, was lowered into the grave amid a prayer that a loving God would have taken his soul to care for an eternity.

"His death won't be in vain," Logan said to the group. "We knew some, or all of us, wouldn't make it home, yet we still came, and now we realize these people are the innocents, being victimized for their beliefs, their land, and their existence. Those of you who want to leave, can, because the fighting is going to a more personal level. Those of us who stay, are staying to protect these people and their way of life."

Shelby had a tree branch and scraped a line in the dirt, twenty feet long. His leg locked up once but a quick poke in the knee popped it loose.

"All right," Logan said. "Those who want to leave, with all of you getting everything promised, and no hard feelings, go to the other side of the line Shelby made. Those who are going to stay and fight for the lives of these people because, Goddammit, no one should have to live in fear for their lives because a religious militia, hired by a government, are going to kill, rape, and destroy their homes and villages," he paused a moment, taking a breath, "stay where you are."

Logan gave them five minutes to decide. South of the line was empty. "Manny would be proud," he said, quietly.

Chapter Twenty-One

The next morning, Logan and Prescott took a test flight in the helicopter. After climbing, swooping, going into dives and making tight circles with gaining and losing altitude, Prescott announce the copter was fit. They landed as several men approached them, carrying a tarp-covered weapon.

"What have you got there, Logan?" Prescott asked, eyeing the men removing the tarp.

"Say hello to a M-61Vulcan. You probably saw them in Vietnam, didn't you?"

"A Gatling gun. You bet I saw 'em. They're about the nastiest machine gun ever built. Where we gonna put it?"

"I wanted it on a truck, but since the copter is good, we'll mount it on a rail so we can slide it side to side and fire it out of either cargo door. It's going to rock and roll your old bird, you know," Logan said. He stroked the six-barreled, electric motor driven, 100 round a second, machine gun. "This cost a fortune to buy, and the ten thousand rounds were just as expensive, but it'll be worth every dollar. Those 20mm rounds will blow the absolute hell out of the Janjaweed. I should have brought it out earlier, things might be a little different now."

"Logan," Aafreen called to him. "Can you come here?" She motioned to a hut she stood by.

He told Prescott to help with the mounting, and walked to the hut. Inside, one of the natives sat with the elder, talking in soft voices. The elder stood up with the native and said, "This is a man you asked me to find. His name is Haueli, he takes care of the livestock."

Logan introduced himself and shook the man's hand. "Shelby's lady is a distant relative to a famous man, General Black Jack Pershing. She told me a story about him when he fought Muslims in the Philippines back in the early 1900's. He came up with a unique strategy for defeating them. "Here's what I want from you, Haueli."

After fifteen minutes of talk, Logan came out of the hut and waved a middle aged soldier over to him. "Ralph, I want you to take a cargo truck, that native over there, and run an errand for me. It's going to take you a couple of days. Be careful, don't tell anyone what you'll have on the truck and don't engage the Arabs."

* * *

"All right, here's the plan, simple as it sounds," Logan told the men gathered near the helicopter. "We're taking the war to the Janjaweed, starting now." A murmuring of approval came from the soldiers. "Once the Vulcan is mounted and ready, we'll have the copter blow the hell out of them from a distance. Alfred, you've fired it before so you go with Prescott. Archie," he said to an older soldier, "you handle the reloading and tell us what the Janjaweed are doing to get away. Questions?" he asked. No one had any.

"Now, the rest of us, except the natives and two of our men, will take the trucks and wait a mile or so away for the copter to attack. When it does, all hell should be breaking loose and after Archie here tells us where they're heading, we'll intercept and take them out." Logan looked to the direction of Manny's grave. "We want to stay far enough away so that any shooting they do will be lucky to come close to us. Make sure, I repeat, make sure you've all got your flak jackets on, and put the ceramic plates in. Any questions or comments?"

"How late can it be if we're gonna do it today?" One soldier asked.

"We don't want the helicopter flying in the dark, so I'd say two, at the latest. They've got three hours to have the bird ready," Logan said. "Get your equipment ready and try to rest a little. I'll let you know by one."

Logan kept pestering Prescott and the men installing the Gatling gun until he was finally told to go take a walk until they got a hold of him. Prescott walked up to him at 3:15. "She's ready," he said.

"It's too late now, I've already told the men to stand down. We'll take off in the trucks at sunrise, and you follow about a half hour later. The whole situation depends on you firing on them from a safe distance and we'll kill the laggards. With the Vulcan, they're gonna know we aren't fooling around. I want to kill as many of them as possible," Logan said. A small smile crept onto his face. "They aren't going to expect this kind of fire power. Exciting, isn't it?"

"I don't know about exciting, but we're sure as hell going to enlighten them some, I'd imagine," Prescott replied.

"Get some rest, I have a feeling it's going to be an interesting, tough day," Logan said. He passed the word to the rest of the troops. Sunrise, we attack.

* * *

After getting the word, Alfred went to Cabriol's hut. Her mother, Grace saw him and said she was going to get some water and visit her other daughter.

"Tomorrow we take the fight to the Janjaweed," he said, putting his arms around her. "We haven't known each other long, but when this is over, I want to stay here and be with you."

She kissed him. "Alfred, those are my thoughts, too. I love you, and want to spend what time we have together." She went to the fire and took a kettle off a hanger, then poured tea into two cups.

Alfred took the cup and sipped some, then said, "We will have a long time together. It feels right, coming back to my Sudanese roots. Once we take out the Janjaweed, our life will be glorious, I promise you."

She closed the hut's opening, took his cup and set it by the fire, then guided him to the bed of blankets. "I never imagined I would find a man like you," she murmured, pulling him down on top of her.

"Are you sure about this? We haven't known each other very long and I don't want you to think I'm taking advantage of you."

"No, believe me, you're not. Who knows if we will be alive tomorrow, next week or at year's end," she whispered.

* * *

Logan met with Jean Paul in a small hut near the edge of the village. Jean Paul took a small bottle of whiskey out of his duffle bag, two paper cups, and poured a small amount in each, before handing one of the cups to his friend.

"I have to keep telling myself we're really here, killing men and losing a good man of ours. It's quite surreal. However, Logan, I am indebted to you for saving my family, the village, and everyone in it. I will also live the rest of my life regretting the loss of Manny and wondering if it will be worth it, especially if anyone else dies."

"Jean Paul, I want you to listen and remember what I'm going to tell you. Every one of us, with possibly the exception of you, knew the risks, knew that we can all die here. But, as you said, *however*, we have accepted that possibility because we're soldiers. I'm not proud to say this, but I know that Shelby and I feel like we're alive again. Adrenalin rush is a drug we need every so often. To be honest with you, right now, I'd rather be doing this than anything else, and probably every man here feels the same."

He finished the whiskey and held the cup out. "One more for the road, if you don't mind," Logan said with a tight smile. "And one question for you."

Jean Paul nodded as he poured the whiskey into the cups. "Fire away."

"You said you might wonder if it will be worth it if any more die, or something to that effect. What if you hadn't done anything and the Janjaweed burned the village, raped your sisters and mother, and killed all the men?"

Jean Paul didn't say anything at first. He sipped from the cup, his thumb circling the lip. "I'm not going to answer that question, Logan. I want my family and the village to be safe. I want the men who've come here to be safe. No matter the outcome, I'll probably never be sure I've made the right decision. I'm not a warrior or a soldier, God knows sometimes I wish I was one. One thing is definite; seeing what happens to these people, I'm going to do anything I can, spend whatever it takes to help bring peace to them."

"By the way, it looks like Cabriol and Alfred Banjune are becoming involved. Is that okay with you?"

"She's in her forties, old enough to do what she wants without my permission. I am worried about Aafreen, though, with what happened to Omallia. They were close," Jean Paul said. "She's lost some of her spirit, it appears."

"From what I've seen, Aafreen is a strong woman, she'll be okay, I think. One hell of a fighter and a pretty good shot." Logan got to his feet, handing the cup to Jean Paul. "There's a saying in the west that I believe applies to you, Jean Paul."

"And what might that be?"

"You're a man to ride the river with," Logan said softly, then left as Jean Paul's eyes glistened with tears.

"Thank you, Logan."

* * *

Logan walked to every man who was on the perimeter guard line, telling them to be careful and at sunrise they were taking it to the Janjaweed. He also told them he wanted a perimeter farther out and use the goggles. From there he made sure all the other soldiers in the village knew tomorrow was the day their offensive attack would begin, but they had to be ready in case they were attacked tonight.

Prescott stayed in the helicopter, he once had called it his home away from home. Cigarette smoke drifted from the open cockpit window as Logan walked up to the copter. "Permission to enter, captain," he said lightly.

"Wipe your feet and come aboard."

Inside, Prescott put down his MRE and pointed to the co-pilot's seat. "What's up?" he asked, chewing the last of a biscuit.

"Are you ready for tomorrow?"

"You betcha. She's gassed, ammo's loaded, Alfred has the gun sliding nice, and I'm psyched. Any chance they might try to get us tonight?"

"Yeah, possibly. I'm having the guys go further out with the night vision goggles. If the Arabs try a sneak attack we'll be ready," Logan answered.

After leaving the helicopter, he found Aafreen and told her to make sure the natives were armed and ready, especially after dark. "You okay? Jean Paul is worried about you," he asked her.

"I'm surviving. Having someone you thought might be your mate, be a traitor is hard, hard for anyone, don't you agree?" she asked.

"I do, and you're holding up fine considering the circumstances."

"Jean Paul needn't worry about me, Logan. Thank you for asking. I'll make it all right, " she said. "It will just take some time."

"I know. We just need to get this over, and hopefully, after tomorrow, it will be," Logan said. He stroked her hand, and then left the hut.

Tomorrow, so much depended on tomorrow, he thought. We have to hit them and hit them hard. So hard the Janjaweed know they can't raid this village and leave alive. If there's a God, he'll let us kill all of them.

Chapter Twenty-Two

As the sun rose casting long shadows from the east, men loaded weapons and ammo into the trucks before climbing in the back. Few words were spoken other than telling each other to check their gear and rifles.

Logan approached Jean Paul who stood by one of the cargo trucks. "You're staying to help defend the village," he said. "Cranston, over there will be here with you."

"I want to go with the rest of you," Jean Paul replied. "I feel I've proven myself and I insist on going."

Logan put a thumb under his chin, which he did when thinking hard. "You're right, get aboard."

Jean Paul climbed up into the back of the truck while Logan told another soldier to stay with Cranston.

Walking to the helicopter, he asked Alfred and Prescott if they had any questions.

"Nope," Prescott said. "We take off thirty minutes after you leave, stay a safe distance and blow the hell out of them. Fire at our discretion?"

"Yeah, just don't use all your ammo right off. Have the gun set at three-round bursts."

"Got it," Alfred said.

After leaving the copter, Logan went to the caravan of trucks, climbed on the hood of one and hollered for everyone's attention. "We need at least three or four prisoners, ones that aren't shot up too bad." He looked at the sun, slid off the truck and stepped into the UAZ. "Let's hit it."

Engines started and with the UAZ leading, the caravan left the village. Aafreen watched them leave before finding Samantha. "Are you worried for Shelby?"

She nodded her head. "He's such a damn cowboy, you never know what he's going to do. I'm glad he's riding with Logan." Both women had AK-47's on their shoulders, hanging from the slings.

"I hear Logan sent a truck on a mission because of a story about some relative of yours," Aafreen said.

Sam nodded, a smile crossing her face. "My family is distantly related to a famous general, Black Jack Pershing. He was sent to the Philippines in the early 1900's to fight Islamist terrorists."

Aafreen waited as they walked, Sam not saying anything. "Well? What happened?"

"Don't say anything, because it's folklore... never proven or disproved." Sam took Aafreen's hand and guided her to a bunker of sandbags, both sitting down on the bags. Samantha told her story about the general.

* * *

Thirty minutes after the trucks left, Prescott powered the helicopter on, blowing a thick screen of dust and sand as the blades increased speed. The copter lifted off, gained altitude before turning and heading west. Alfred leaned out of a cargo door, waving at Cabriol, who was waving back from the ground. "Get me back alive, my man," Alfred told Prescott, who stuck his thumb up in the air.

The copter gained altitude and flew at three thousand feet, hugging the skyline of faraway mountains. The convoy could be seen working its way toward the Janjaweed camp, where tendrils of smoke from dying camp fires snaked into the air. Men could be seen running toward the horses and camels. Some flashes of gunfire could be seen.

"Steady and ready," Prescott said over the intercom. "Steady... steady... fire when ready." The electric switch to the barrel rotator was flipped, and the Vulcan jolted the copter with every burst. Down on the ground, the 20mm rounds blew tents and men into the air. It looked as if the Arabs were in a panic until one man stood with a rifle, fired at the copter then waved his arms. Men mounted their animals, put them into a run away from the camp, and away from the convoy.

"Logan, they're heading away from you, toward the west," Prescott said.

"Get in front of them and try to make 'em turn around, we're approaching the camp now," Logan replied.

Prescott pushed the helicopter's throttle forward after telling Alfred what they were going to do. The copter's nose lowered as it flew past the riders then made a swooping half turn so the Vulcan pointed at the Janjaweed horsemen. The camel riders had spread out making a fan-like turn back towards the camp.

Alfred squeezed off the bursts of the high explosive incendiary rounds at the men down below, blowing horses and riders into flaming pieces of debris. Alfred quickly had a thought of what hell must be like. He turned the six-barreled cannon toward the camel riders, again firing off three round bursts. Once he changed the selector to ten rounds and shot fifty rounds in fifteen seconds. The remaining camel and horseback riders turned back in the direction of the camp.

* * *

"Spread out, make sure we won't be cross-firing into each other. Here they come," Logan said over the

radio. "Try to get some prisoners, now, hit them hard."
He stood up and began firing the .30 caliber machine
gun that was mounted on the roof of the UAZ.

Shelby saw a man crawling, fifty feet away. "I'll get
us the first one," he said, bailing out of the vehicle and
sprinting to the wounded Arab. He quickly bound his
hands and feet, then looking at Logan, raised his arms
like a cowboy in a rodeo calf roping.

"Goddammit, Shelby, quit screwing around,"
Logan yelled. He turned the machine gun in Shelby's
direction and fired, bringing down two riders who were
bearing down on him.

Shelby turned when the riders fell off their horses.
He grabbed the collar of the fighter he'd tied up and
dragged him to one of the light armored trucks,
throwing him into the open back. "Keep an eye on this
one and bring him back to the village... alive," Shelby
ordered.

One man nodded, took some rope, and tied the
fighter's neck to the bench seat leg on the floor of the
truck. "He'll be okay, don't worry, man."

Shelby jumped back into the UAZ just as Logan
fired at some retreating riders. The ground looked like
the inside of a slaughter house. Blood, body pieces and
bodies lay strewn around them. They could hear the
heavy firing of the Vulcan from the helicopter.

Shelby pointed and said, "Oh, shit!"

* * *

Petro saw the launch. He yelled into his radio, "Lee,
Stinger coming! Stinger coming!"

Everyone with a radio who heard Petro looked up
and saw the smoke trail as the missile homed in on the
helicopter. The copter hovered, not moving.

"Get the hell away," Shelby yelled. "What's he doing?" he shouted at Logan.

A long burst of cannon fire from the copter hit the missile, blowing it into pieces. "We're out of ammo and getting out of here," Prescott radioed. The copter turned as another missile fired up from behind a small cluster of trees.

"Here comes another one," Petro radioed. They watched the helicopter swoop low, and then the missile hit the back rotor. The explosion turned the copter nearly 180 degrees and blew the tail off, putting the helicopter into a slow spin, dropping behind another ridge of sand and out of sight.

"Let's get there," Logan said over the radio. "Petro, you're closest, take the lead... hurry, man."

Petro's truck bucked over the brush heading in the direction of the downed helicopter. A moment later an explosion came from behind the ridge, a huge cloud of smoke and flame rising. "Oh Christ," Petro muttered. "Lee, Alfred." The truck rumbled up the ridge and on the top slammed on its brakes. Below, the entire helicopter was in flames. Janjaweed closed in firing automatic rifles into the wreckage.

The .30 caliber machine gun began firing. Petro swiveled it side to side cutting down the Janjaweed until they saw the truck. Three men in the truck opened fire with their AK's. A half dozen of the Arabs went down, and the others retreated, shooting back as they fled the area.

Another explosion rocked the truck at the same time Logan and Shelby arrived in the UAZ. The helicopter, what was left of it, was below them, completely engulfed in flames.

Another truck pulled up. Jean Paul jumped out and ran to Logan's outfit. "Alfred and Lee, are they....?"

Logan nodded his head. "No way anyone could survive that. They were also being shot at when the copter was on the ground. Your sister... Alfred, I'm so sorry, Jean Paul." He let the sentence drift.

Logan gazed over the battleground. The Janjaweed had disappeared, leaving their dead and wounded. Picking up the radio he said, "Take the live ones, burn the dead."

Chapter Twenty-Three

Back at the village, a wail of pain and heartbreak sounded from Cabriol's hut. Jean Paul came out, tears running down his face. He came up to Logan while wiping his eyes.

"I can't believe how terrible it was telling her about Alfred. And to think we also lost Prescott and Archie, God rest their souls. What are we going to do now?" Jean Paul asked.

"You saw the cargo truck come in, and what it carried?"

"Yes."

Logan smiled. "We're going to see if history repeats itself, see if Black Jack Pershing really knew something." He walked to the UAZ, waited while Jean Paul climbed in, started the engine, and then looked over to Jean Paul "Do you really want to go? I'm warning you, it won't be pretty."

After a few moments of silence, he said, "I'd like to stay with Cabriol. Would you think less of me?"

"God, no, Jean Paul, Go to her, she needs you." Jean Paul climbed back out of the UAZ and looked at Logan with the face of a man who had seen and done things he would regret for the rest of his life.

Shelby, Petro, and most of the men, with four prisoners tied to trees, waited for Logan to park and come over. Behind him, the cargo truck rolled to a stop. Logan looked to the setting sun and shadows spreading over the area. A pit lay behind the prisoners. "Bring one over."

The driver went to the back of the truck and pulled a squealing pig out. He looked to Logan, who nodded. The man shot the pig, took a pail, slit the belly open and with his hand and knife, took the guts out and loaded the pail with entrails and blood.

"Here's where the fun begins," Logan said. He took a bullet and dunked it into the bucket while the prisoners looked on. Loading it into his Glock, he aimed at the Arab to his left and fired. The man's head flew back and his body went slack. A bullet hole was in the center of his forehead.

"Throw him in the pit." When the body was dumped in, Logan took the bucket and spilled some of the pig guts and blood over the body. "Next."

The remaining three Janjaweed began screaming with sheer panic and terror in their voices. As they strained against the ropes holding them to the trees, Logan again went through the dunking of a single bullet into the pail. He leveled it at the next man and pulled the trigger at the same time the man screamed.

Darkness silently eased over the clearing. Torches and a bonfire were lit, casting eerily shadows over the group. The two bodies lay in the pit, which was about two feet deep.

The third men said in English, "Please, don't. I'll do anything for you if you won't touch me with pig's blood or guts. Kill me, but with dignity. Americans are merciful, I know this for a fact."

His eyes bulged just before the bullet hit him. Like the other two, his body was thrown into the pit, pig guts and blood poured over the body.

"Guess you know according to the Koran, all of you are automatically barred from Paradise, even if you die a martyr, due to porcine 'contamination'. But, you don't need me to tell you that, do you? We're giving you a snack to enjoy on the way to Hell." Logan tipped the bucket so the remaining man could see him soak his bullet in the blood and fat. The man fought against the ropes, spittle flew out of his mouth as he first cursed, then prayed for himself.

Logan slid the bullet into the Glock, wiped his hand, then pulled the trigger. The bullet hit three inches above the head of the Janjaweed. "Tell them, this is what will happen to every one of you who attacks us or the village again. Tell them." He turned away. "Cut him loose."

When the ropes were cut off, the man turned and ran into the darkness. "Probably get to his camp in the morning. It will be interesting," Logan said, watching the man disappear. "Brannigan, set up a perimeter around the village. "We'll hit them again in the daylight."

* * *

At first, Shelby didn't believe what he saw. A horse, carrying two men with their hands raised into the air, walked into the clearing.

"Don't shoot, don't shoot. It's Alfred and Lee," Alfred yelled. When he saw who the men were, both slid from the horse and staggered to the soldiers.

Shelby helped Prescott, who had a difficult time walking. "We thought you guys were dead," Shelby said, then called on the radio to have Molly stand by at the village. They were helped into the back of a truck, Shelby, Petro and Logan climbed in beside them.

They saw two men with burns over their bodies and gashes oozing blood through crude bandages. Logan gave them water, poured some over their burns, then said, " What about Archie? How did you make it out, we saw the helicopter on fire after the explosion." The truck was heading back to the village as fast as possible.

Alfred took a long pull from the water bottle, wiped his lips with the back of his hand, then took another swallow. Prescott drank, then coughed, blood ran down his chin. "I think Lee's got some lung damage," Alfred said. He put his hand up. "After we get Lee to Molly. What about Cabriol?"

Logan shook his head. "We thought we'd lost the three of you. She was told."

"Archie died in the helicopter. Shrapnel from the missile hit got him."

"We'll talk later," Logan said as the truck rolled into the village. Molly and Samantha stood by, a large medicine bag between them.

Alfred and Prescott were helped out of the truck and taken to the two women, who immediately began checking them. Molly ordered Prescott onto a stretcher and he was taken to the first aid hut. Alfred said he could walk and as he started after Prescott, heard a scream.

"Alfred, Alfred, oh my God!" Cabriol screamed again. She ran through the villagers and threw her arms around him. She stepped back. "You're hurt," she blurted out. "Did I hurt you?"

"No, no, I'm so happy to see you I couldn't feel any pain. Come with me to the hut," Alfred said, putting an arm carefully around her shoulders. "You can hold my hand," he laughed, putting her hand in his. They followed Prescott.

* * *

A half an hour passed with no one coming out of the first aid hut. "Go talk to him, Logan, find out how they made it," Shelby said, walking in a circle. "Unbelievable, I saw the helicopter get hit and on the ground burning."

"They obviously survived, except Archie... here he comes," Logan said, moving aside so Alfred and Cabriol could join them. "Okay," he said to Alfred, "How's Lee and how did you guys make it out of the helicopter?"

Alfred's face and arms were smeared in burn ointment, bandages covered his face, arms and his chest. He didn't have a shirt on. "Molly said the deepest burns had to be bandaged, the rest will heal. Fortunately no third degree. Lee has a punctured lung and burns, no third degree either."

"We'll take you to the nearest hospital," Logan said.

"No, Molly says we'll live." He smiled at Cabriol, squeezed her shoulders gently, then began. "When we were hit with the missile, the only thing Lee could do was keep the copter leveled as it fell. Poor old Archie was killed from a chunk of fuselage that caught him in head after the missile got us. The only thing we could do was bail out after the copter hit the ground."

Alfred's eyes filled with moisture. "God, we didn't want to leave Archie, but we knew there was only a couple of seconds to get out of the copter. We jumped out and were running towards a thicket of bad-ass brush when the helicopter exploded." He paused, taking a deep breath. "Here's the part that's unbelievable. The blast threw us about fifteen feet in the air and we landed in the thicket. Man, we heard 'em shooting but didn't dare move in case they didn't know we were out of the bird.

We stayed there about an hour, made sure there wasn't any Janjaweed around, crawled out and started walking for the village. I was helping Lee and thought we couldn't make it back, then I saw the horse. The rider was lying there dead, the reins tied around his hand. I think that's why the horse hadn't run off, couldn't shake the guy loose. So we got the reins, got on the horse and here we are."

"You don't know how glad we are to see you both alive," Logan said. He told Alfred about the pig guts and blood with the prisoners. "We're going to attack the camp tomorrow and finish this."

* * *

Sunrise found the trucks moving towards the Janjaweed camp in a wedge formation. Orders were to fire on sight and if the Arabs tried riding around them, they would be able to fire on them without putting their trucks and men in a crossfire. The closer they came the more tense the men became. Hands tightened on the stocks of the rifles. Shelby carried a RPG while Petro in the truck manned one of the .30 caliber machine guns and Logan in the UAZ, the other .30 caliber. Jean Paul rode with Logan gripping his AK-47, sweat already beading on his forehead.

They came up the ridge before the camp and everyone stopped at the top. No smoke from campfires, tents gone or remnants lying on the ground, no horses or camels. The camp was completely deserted. Logan had two men climb a higher ridge to scan the area with binoculars. Having the men spread out, ready for an ambush, he waited until the two men came back down.

"Nothing," the soldier, whose name was Hastings, reported. "There ain't an Arab to be killed," he said.

"All right, we'll continue east, see if we can find them," Logan ordered, climbing back into his vehicle.

Three hours later, they were fifteen miles further east from the camp. They followed tracks made from horses and camels. Several of Logan's men scouted more than a mile north and south for tracks, and didn't find any.

* * *

The sun was an hour from setting when the convoy rolled back into the village. Logan set up a perimeter guard, and told the men, "We'll give it a week. If they don't come back, I think the village will be safe." He looked up to the sky. "Thanks, Black Jack."

* * *

During the week, Alfred told Logan he was staying with Cabriol, in the village. "This is where I belong, with Cabriol and my homeland," he said. Logan gave them his blessings.

Jean Paul promised help in maintaining communications and supplies with the village. He tried unsuccessfully to have his mother, Cabriol, and Aafreen come back to the states with him, and was secretly pleased Alfred was staying with his younger sister. He was a very good man.

Alfred promised Logan they would always have pigs in the village. After he had been told of General Pershing's method for putting down the Muslim terrorists in the Philippines, he just smiled and shook his head. "Don't worry, Logan, we'll be fine, and thank you."

At the end of the week in two trucks, the soldiers took only their personal weapons and extra ammo for the trip to the abandoned airstrip. The rest of the ammunition, MRE's, AK-47's, RPG's, .30 caliber machine guns and trucks, were left for the villagers. Aafreen promised with Alfred they would remain alert and cautious. Logan radioed the pilots to be ready for takeoff when they arrived, in approximately four hours.

After hugs, laughter and tears, the Americans left, hoping to God the Janjaweed were gone for good.

* * *

The trip to the airfield was uneventful. Two natives, who were taught to drive, came along and left for the village in the two trucks.

The jet lifted from the airport with several feet to spare, and once in the air, whiskey, wine and beer was served to the soldiers. Most drank until they passed out. Those that didn't drink, slept.

Eighteen hours later, they landed at a private airport in New Jersey. Jean Paul shook every man's hand and gave out checks, double the amount originally agreed. He asked everyone to keep in contact with him and if they needed anything to contact him. When Molly reached him, he hugged and thanked her, along with offering her a job working with vets. She smiled and kissed him on the cheek, saying she would be in touch.

* * *

"I owe you all so much more," Jean Paul said to Shelby, Petro, and Samantha, the next day. Logan sat next to him in his office at WBS "You saved my family and their village. Logan and I have talked; we would like to offer you jobs, working for the company."

Petro immediately said yes, Samantha also. Shelby smiled and said, "I'll have to think it over. Those elephant poachers in Kenya are really pissing me off."

"That's my Shelby," Logan said.

Epilogue --Six months later

They met at the Breckenridge Steak House, on West 59th and 41st, in Manhattan. Petro and Samantha sat sipping wine as Logan and Jean Paul walked into the restaurant. They sat down at the table and ordered a drink.

"I've talked to Aafreen every week. No sign of the Janjaweed. What an ancestor you had," Jean Paul said. "How are you two doing? I don't see you as much as I would like to."

"Marriage is great" Petro said. "Right?"

"Yes, you're the best, or at least you keep telling me," Samantha said. Her features were soft and her face glowed. "Our transfer to the L.A. office has been approved, we leave at the end of the month. Thank you, I heard you personally took care of it."

Petro excused himself for a bathroom run.

"You two deserve it. I have to ask, what happened to you and Shelby?"

She took a deep breath. "He can't settle down. After a couple of weeks he was looking into, what he called, an adventure, though he wouldn't tell me what. One morning I woke up and he was gone, just a note saying he was sorry and loved me, but he couldn't settle down. I haven't heard from him since."

Petro returned, setting down. His mouth dropped open. "Look," he said, pointing to the television on the wall. There was a picture behind the commentator of several, obviously dead, black men. Stacked on top of them were several elephant tusks.

"This is Ronald Jacobs reporting for CNN. Six bodies of men believed to be elephant poachers were found dead today in the Kenya Elephant reserve. The men had several elephant tusks piled on top of them. This lends to the rumor about a group of reported Americans taking on the poachers. Notes have been left on the bodies of these men and others previously killed in the last five months. The notes have said, 'Look out, Butch Cassidy is here.'" Jacobs took his glasses off and looked into the camera. "The last note left said, 'Sundance, I could use a hand, no pun intended.' No one has any idea what this means.'" Jacobs put his glasses back on and stared into the camera, lifting a fist. "Save the elephants. Goodnight and stay tuned for sports."

Jean Paul looked at Logan with a gleam in his eyes. He took a sip of wine and said, "So, does the saga continue?"

Logan smiled as he raised his glass. "Maybe, now that the rebel has a cause."

THE END